THE PENGUIN CLASSICS

FOUNDER EDITOR (1944–64): E. V. RIEU

ALPHONSE DAUDET was born at Nîmes in 1840. He is chiefly remembered today for *Letters from my Windmill*, which appeared in *Le Figaro* in 1866, and for his Tartarin novels, a sequence of burlesque tales of Provençal life. He also wrote several naturalistic novels about the contemporary business, social and political scene, as well as the play *L'Arlésienne* for which Bizet composed the incidental music.

Daudet was also active in public life, becoming private secretary to the Duc de Morny, Napoleon III's half-brother and minister. He served in the *Garde Nationale* during the Franco-Prussian war, which he survived to live until 1897.

FREDERICK DAVIES is widely known as the translator of the plays of Carlo Goldoni. His *Four Comedies* by Goldoni and his *Three French Farces* have been published in the Penguin Classics. He is a Fellow Commoner of Churchill College.

EDWARD ARDIZZONE was born in 1900 and studied art at Westminster and the Central Schools of Art. He was the Official War Artist from 1940 to 1946 and has illustrated over 170 books, including classics by Thackeray and Dickens. He was awarded the C.B.E. in 1971, became a Royal Academician in 1970 and was made a Royal Designer for Industry by the Royal Society of Artists in 1974.

ALPHONSE DAUDET

Letters from my Windmill

TRANSLATED WITH AN INTRODUCTION
BY FREDERICK DAVIES

ILLUSTRATED BY
EDWARD ARDIZZONE

PENGUIN BOOKS

Penguin Books Ltd, Harmondsworth, Middlesex, England
Penguin Books, 40 West 23rd Street, New York, New York 10010, U.S.A.
Penguin Books Australia Ltd, Ringwood, Victoria, Australia
Penguin Books Canada Ltd, 2801 John Street, Markham, Ontario, Canada L3R 1B4
Penguin Books (N.Z.) Ltd, 182–190 Wairau Road, Auckland 10, New Zealand

—

This translation first published 1978
Reprinted 1984

—

Copyright © Frederick Davies, 1978
Illustrations copyright © Edward Ardizzone, 1978
All rights reserved

—

Made and printed in Singapore by
Richard Clay (SE Asia) Pte Ltd
Set in Monotype Ehrhardt

TO GEORGE STEINER

Eloquent and wise interpreter
of man to man

CONTENTS

CONTENTS

INTRODUCTION

Letters from my Windmill and *Tartarin of Tarascon* are now
the only books by Daudet at all widely known outside his
own country. As a result, he has become identified with
them. This not only unjustly circumscribes his achievement; it must inevitably detract from a full appreciation of
Letters from my Windmill. This introduction, therefore,
while incidentally containing information which should en-
hance a reading of the *Letters*, aims at giving a brief account
of Daudet's life and achievement without which the reader
can hardly appreciate to the full the qualities which make
this early book one of Daudet's best.

Between 1875 and 1890, Daudet was the most successful
novelist in France. Furthermore, in the opinion of Edmund
Gosse and other men of letters, he was then the leading
novelist in the world. Today, his books are largely unread.
He has become one of the casualties of literature. Apart
from Anatole France, it is difficult to think of any French
literary figure of such international eminence during his life
whose reputation has suffered such an eclipse since his
death. The reasons are many and complex. Before examining those relevant to Daudet in particular, one which must
certainly have contributed to the neglect of both Daudet and
France during the first half of this century should be mentioned. Both authors are primarily tellers of tales, and since
the advent of psychology the telling of a story has tended to
be regarded as of less importance than the development of
character. In 1927, E. M. Forster declared that in a novel
the story has no intrinsic aesthetic value: it is merely a
support for 'finer growths'. This stricture may now be becoming less sacrosanct, as the recent increasing general and

academic interest in the novels of John Cowper Powys, another great teller of tales for long neglected, tends to suggest. If this be so, the time is ripe for a reconsideration of both Alphonse Daudet and Anatole France.

In the following pages an attempt will be made to present the case for and against Alphonse Daudet, the teller of tales; to explain why Daudet, who had an international reputation during his lifetime as a short-story writer, a dramatist, and novelist, who numbered Flaubert, Zola, Dickens and Henry James among his admirers, who had financially one of the most successful literary careers of the nineteenth century, has largely ceased to be read during this century. It will plead that the best of Daudet deserves to be read as much as and more than the least of Flaubert.

Alphonse Daudet was born at Nîmes in Provence in 1840. His childhood until the age of nine was an extremely happy one: it was these years which gave him his lifelong love for the countryside and people of Provence. In 1849, his father, a silk manufacturer, lost his money and the family moved from the sunshine of Provence to the fogs of Lyons where until the age of sixteen Alphonse's boyhood became more and more depressing and miserable: it was these years which constantly led him to regret his father's failure in life and to care until her death for his mother, who became the victim of her husband's capricious and deeply embittered moods. In 1856, at the age of sixteen, Alphonse had to leave the Lycée in Lyons, abandoning what promised to be a brilliant academic career, in order to support himself as an usher in the college at Alais in the Cévennes. There, his work, which consisted mainly of supervising fifty twelve- to fourteen-year-old boys at their studies, soon proved intolerable to him owing to his sensitive nature and to his shortness of both stature and sight: the memory of this year remained with him all his life and years later he would wake up in the middle of the night dreaming he was still at Alais, saying to himself: 'My God, what are they going to do to me next?' On 1 November 1857, he left Alais to join his elder brother, Ernest, in Paris: and so began the powerful love–hate sentiment Daudet felt for Paris for the rest of his life.

After a train journey of forty-eight hours in a crowded, wooden compartment, he arrived at the Gare de Lyon, a shabby figure with long, blue, cotton socks showing above his goloshes, which he wore not to protect his shoes but because he had no shoes. In his pockets he had only the proverbial forty sous. Supported by his brother, three years older than himself, who had obtained a job as a reporter on the *Spectateur* (and was later to become well known as a political writer and historian), Alphonse began searching for a publisher for the poems he had written at Lyons and at Alais. After six months he not only found one, but, more remarkable still, he found one who was prepared to publish the book at his own expense.

Les Amoureuses, though it hardly sold at all, had an immediate success in literary circles and at the age of eighteen Daudet gained entrance to all the literary salons of Paris. The poems attracted the approval of the Empress, wife of Napoleon III, at whose instigation the Emperor's half-brother, the Duc de Morny, President of the Corps Législatif, appointed Daudet as one of his secretaries. This government appointment, while not a sinecure, gave him a large amount of leisure-time for the pursuit of his literary ambitions and relieved him from being an expense to his brother. It also enabled him, as his brother was later to write, 'to enter every low haunt of Bohemia'. It was during these years that Daudet, as he himself revealed to Edmond de Goncourt, must have contracted the dormant syphilis which in his early forties entered into its third stage of locomotor ataxy and gave him intense pain and suffering until his death at the age of fifty-seven.

Daudet's literary ambitions at this time were directed towards the stage, for which he wrote five full-length plays none of which was successful at its first production, not even *L'Arlésienne* for which Bizet wrote the incidental music. Later, of course, he adapted some of his successful novels for the stage where they proved equally successful, as did *L'Arlésienne* when it was revived in 1885. But it was the cool reception given to his plays at this time, especially to the first production of *L'Arlésienne*, which decided Daudet to turn to the novel, and in 1874 he published *Fromont jeune et Risler aîné* which had an immediate and great success.

The privations Daudet had suffered during his first two years in Paris undermined his health and the Duc de Morny allowed him several leaves of absence from Paris. He revisited his native Provence and gathered much of the material he was to use in *Letters from my Windmill*. He visited Corsica, as may be seen from three of the stories in this book, 'The Lighthouse of *Les Sanguinaires*', 'The Agony of *La Sémillante*', and 'The Customs Men'. And it is to his visit to Algeria that we owe 'At Milianah', 'The Locusts' and 'The Oranges'.

Among other events which influenced Daudet during his early career was his service as a soldier in the National Guard during the siege of Paris, an experience to which we owe such perfect short stories as 'La Dernière Classe' in his *Contes du Lundi*, as well as 'Barrack-room Memories', the last of the *Letters from my Windmill*.

In 1867 Daudet married Julia Allard. Their married life was one of great happiness. His wife calmed his excitable temperament, served him often as a wise and helpful collaborator, and eased his later life of pain and ill-health. It was also a marriage of intellectual harmony: Madame Daudet herself wrote and published several books.

The year before his marriage there had appeared in the Paris journal *L'Evénement* the first of the *Letters from my*

Windmill, written under the influence of his close friend, Frédéric Mistral, the Provençal poet, and, at first, in collaboration with a young Parisian friend also from Provence named Paul Arène. Then followed in 1868 the first of his longer works, *Le Petit Chose*, a semi-autobiographical story which contained many details of his early life. In 1872 appeared *Les Aventures prodigieuses de Tartarin de Tarascon*, as well as the three-act tragedy *L'Arlésienne*, whose failure determined Daudet to abandon the stage for fiction. In 1874, with *Fromont jeune et Risler aîné*, Daudet published his first full-length novel and became immediately the most widely read and successful author of the day. When the novel proved such an immense success, his publisher tore up the contract and made out a new one four times as advantageous to the author.

There followed *Jack* (1876), *Le Nabab* (1877), *Les Rois en exil* (1879), *Numa Roumestan* (1881), *L'Evangéliste* (1883), *Sapho* (1884), *Tartarin sur les Alpes* (1885), *L'Immortel* (1888), *Port Tarascon* (1890). For the most part they all portray the Paris that Daudet knew so well, and even people whom he knew personally. Daudet took little care to conceal his sources, sometimes even using people's real names. It is not difficult to understand why he, who wanted to please so much, should have made so many enemies. It was, also, on the grounds of Daudet's meticulous observation, his use of notebooks which he filled with visual impressions and true experiences, that Zola tried to claim him as a fellow member of the naturalist school. But it must be obvious to the most superficial reader that the undoubted naturalistic element in Daudet's novel is owing to purely fortuitous circumstances of time and place, and to his own realization that what he lacked in imagination he had to make up for by minute observation of real life. At heart Daudet is a son of Provence, with all the Provençal's love of sunshine and laughter and poetry. Like Georges Simenon today, he is an idealist attracted towards the sordid themes of naturalism by his immense sympathy with life's failures – *les ratés* – rather than by any pseudo-scientific literary theory such as Zola tried to propagate.

What is strikingly obvious in all Daudet's work and especially in *Letters from my Windmill* is that he could never reconcile his love–hate for Paris with his deep almost umbilical attachment to Provence. Within the first few lines of the first letter in this book, we find Daudet comparing the two – to the detriment of Paris: 'Why then should you wish me to regret Paris, your noisy, dirty Paris? It is so perfect here in my mill! . . .' And the theme comes full-circle in the last lines of the last letter: 'My Paris haunts me here, just as yours does . . . And it seems to me, as I lie in the grass, aching with the pain of my memories, that I am seeing in the sound of that receding drum, all my Paris passing between the pines . . . Oh, Paris! . . . Paris! . . . Always Paris!'

When Daudet was in Paris, his thoughts turned continually to Provence. In the *Memoirs* of Léon Daudet, his son relates how, in order to give himself the illusion he was back in Provence, his father used to go every week to a shop in the rue Turbigo called 'Aux Produits du Midi' where he would fill his and his son's pockets with all kinds of the products of Provence.

And when Daudet was in Provence, his thoughts turned constantly to Paris. Once this is realized, it can be seen that all his writing life was a preparation for his treatment of this theme in what he considered to be his best novel: *Numa Roumestan*. In *Numa Roumestan* he set out to explore the contrast between the southern and the northern temperament and character. He had already touched on this theme in much of his work, especially in *Le Petit Chose* and *Le Nabab*. In *Numa Roumestan*, it becomes central, explicit and totally dynamic: the passionate Provençal temperament and imagination is shown to be both opposite and incomprehensible to the cool rationalism and sang-froid of the Parisian. Whenever and wherever the two meet there must inevitably be misunderstanding and suffering. The plot of *Numa Roumestan*, based on this theme, concerns the marriage of a French politician, born and with his roots still deep in Provence, to a Parisian woman. The resulting discords are revealed, at first with delicate insight, and then with mounting dramatic intensity. Throughout the entire novel Daudet moves effortlessly between the seamy grandeur of Paris and the sunny gaiety of Provence. It was the book he had been preparing all his life to write.

Nevertheless, it has been criticized on the grounds that, while it is about the life of a politician, it is not a political novel. The character and personality of Numa are revealed in great depth and with great detail but we are told little about his political ideas. It is easy to criticize a novelist for not having written the novel he should have written; and it is possible also that Daudet wished to emphasize the ideological void of political life in France at the time. The more likely explanations are that Daudet had little interest in politics, and that it was the personal not the political life of Numa he was concerned with. Few readers can fail to be moved by the passions and human problems of this novel. It was and is Daudet's most impressive achievement.

In England, Edmund Gosse hailed it as a major work of art. George Meredith wrote: 'Read *Numa Roumestan* if you can lay your hand on it. I do not care for the other novels of Daudet but this is a consummate piece of work.' Henry James expressed himself even more enthusiastically: '*Numa Roumestan* is a masterpiece; it is really a perfect work; it has no weaknesses; it is a compact and harmonious whole.'

And so we return to the problem: why, since then, has Daudet's reputation so declined?

Some of the reasons are discernible during his lifetime.

Even when he was an international celebrity his books were the subject of passionate controversy. The chief accusations brought against him were plagiarism, excess of sentimentality, lack of imagination, and anti-Semitism.

The charge of plagiarism rested chiefly on the extent to which Arène had collaborated with Daudet in the first series of the *Letters from my Windmill*, and on the resemblances between Daudet's novels and those of Dickens.

In 1883, seventeen years after his collaboration with Daudet in the first series of *Letters from my Windmill* for the journal, *L'Evénement*, Paul Arène claimed an extensive share in the authorship of the complete stories which had been first published in book form in 1869 and republished in 1879. His claim was immediately seized upon by Daudet's enemies who went so far as to suggest that the whole book was actually the work of Arène.

The facts are these. A series of twelve letters was published in *L'Evénement*, beginning in the autumn of 1866. A second series was published in *Le Figaro* in 1868, after Daudet's marriage. The first five letters of the first series were signed 'Marie-Gaston', a double-pseudonym chosen by Daudet and Arène to indicate their joint authorship; the sixth letter was signed 'Alphonse Daudet', with 'Marie-Gaston' in parenthesis below; the remaining letters were signed simply 'Alphonse Daudet'. All the letters of the second series were signed 'Alphonse Daudet'.

The most charitable explanation of Arène's charge is that seventeen years after their collaboration Arène knew he was incapable of becoming, as Daudet had become, a great popular writer, and he began to complain to his fellow-loafers in the Paris cafés where he spent most of his time that he had been robbed. This malicious but perhaps understandable accusation was seized upon by those critics who were only too glad to be able to vent their spleen against a popular writer.

It was these critics also who insisted on emphasizing the resemblances between Daudet's novels and Dickens's. They searched for specific parallels between the characters portrayed by the two novelists. This was especially the case with *Le Petit Chose*, which became known as Daudet's 'Copperfield', its author being christened 'the Dickens of France'. Daudet consistently maintained that when he wrote *Le Petit Chose* he had never read a novel by Dickens, and after Dickens himself had read the book he went out of his way to show a warmly benevolent interest in the young French writer, referring to him as 'my little brother in France'. Again, when *Tartarin de Tarascon* was published, the opportunity was quickly seized by these critics to point out the resemblances with *The Pickwick Papers*. This also was a forced comparison of superficial resemblances. *Tartarin de Tarascon* is laughter for its own sake, its hero too absurd a figure, too much the object of mockery, for any meaningful comparison with the comic but lovable, slightly silly but completely human, figure of Mr Pickwick.

Daudet made his own comment on these accusations in his *Trente ans de Paris* where he attributes the fortuitous resemblances between himself and Dickens to their kindred temperaments and sympathies, to the similarity of their early life and the misfortune and poverty that blighted their childhood, and to the bitter struggle of their young manhood which gave to them both their deep sympathy with human suffering. This understanding of suffering, especially the suffering of 'childhood lost in the misery of great towns', is certainly a strong affinity between the two writers and many of the characters of their novels are frequently exaggerated under this stimulus. But their true affinity lies in the ability of both to combine humour and pathos, to arouse laughter and tears.

Before considering the following two pieces of deductive reasoning, whose conclusions make it very unlikely that

Daudet was ever consciously guilty of plagiarism, it is worth noting that Flaubert was also accused of plagiarism on the grounds that before he wrote *Bouvard et Pécuchet* he had read a short story called *Les Deux Greffiers* whose plot bears a striking resemblance to that of *Bouvard et Pécuchet*.

The evidence, from Daudet's notebooks and manuscripts, is overwhelming that in all his work he tried to apply the highest standards of artistic integrity. That the maintenance of such standards was of the greatest importance to him is shown not only in the whole of *Le Petit Chose*, but also in many of the letters in the present book. Furthermore, it is certain that Daudet worked in some form of collaboration all his life. Before his marriage he relied upon the help and advice of his elder brother, and after, of his wife. But what he was never known to do was to collaborate in the working-out of someone else's ideas. It is obvious that, as with Labiche and Feydeau, this need for a sympathetic hearing and moral support was deeply rooted in his character, and that we may safely assume, as with Labiche and Feydeau, that Daudet alone was the creator.

The second accusation brought against Daudet – an excess of sentimentality – can be justified. So it can against Dickens. But the label of sentimentality is not therefore applied indiscriminately and with condemnation to all Dickens's work. Neither should it be to Daudet's. In Daudet's best work – in the present book, in *Le Petit Chose*, *Numa Roumestan* and other works – the sentimental strain is kept under artistic control. In these works it is not a flaw but an asset, not a weakness but a strength: it is, to a great extent, what should give these works their enduring appeal.

That this strength could become a weakness was always inherent in Daudet's deliberately cultivated style of *littérature debout*. The danger was that such a style, which depended so much on the warmth and charm of the writer's engaging tone of voice, could easily deteriorate into a direct emotional appeal to the reader, into a facile tug at the heart-strings. Dickens was frequently guilty of this: he found his readers liked pathos; so he gave it them. Today the death of Little Nell repels; yet that does not cause Dickens to be condemned as sentimental and left unread. And because today the death of Desirée Delobelle in *Fromont jeune et Risler aîné* repels, it should not cause Daudet to be condemned as sentimental and left unread. Moreover, Daudet never sentimentalizes his bad characters. He shows great pity for them but always a far greater measure of pity for their victims. But, of course, in this respect, Daudet is at odds with much of modern fiction, from Proust to Graham Greene, which tends to avoid concern for and even interest in the good and to lavish them on the ruthless and depraved.

With regard to the third accusation, Daudet himself used to concede, not without pride, that he lacked imagination. All he wrote, he maintained, was drawn from life: 'to invent for him was to remember'. But he used not only his memory and his notebooks to make up for what he may have lacked in imagination. He used what was probably the more indispensable of his two greatest assets as a writer: his great gift of empathy, his sensitivity, his hypersensitive aware-ness, his ability to convey with vivid immediacy the feel, the texture, the unique otherness, of people, places and things. In his late *Notes sur la vie* he says with the insight into himself which was but another aspect of his great sensitivity, 'What a marvellous machine for feeling I was, especially when I was very young ... How porous and penetrable I must have been: impressions, sensations enough to fill a pile of books, and all with dream-like intensity.'

Yet here again the critics seem, almost deliberately, to have missed the point; it was invention that Daudet lacked rather than imagination. And it was the nature of his imagination which led, many French critics astray. Daudet found it difficult to invent: he had to begin with real people and places he had known personally. Then his imagination could begin to work, and, as with Dickens, his imagination tended often towards exaggeration. His imagination was such that he was prone to embellish the real in order to make it more piquant, more pathetic, or more picturesque. As a result, he was accused of inaccuracies, deliberate omissions and distortions. The most obvious example of this is in the preface, first published as an article in the *Nouvelle Révue*, which he wrote for a later edition of *Letters from my Windmill*. In this he was unable to confess that his windmill had not been a ruin. So he compromised, describing the windmill as he had done in the letters, and adding the suggestion that it had later been restored. He states, as well, that as soon as he arrived at Montauban he would whistle to one of the dogs to accompany him up to his windmill. Daudet detested dogs and had always been extremely frightened of them ever since he had been attacked by a mad dog when he was a child.

The fourth accusation, that he was anti-Semitic, though it does not merit any valid place in an estimate of Daudet's artistic achievement, is still brought against him. Yet there is nothing in all his books nor in the people he associated with that can lend support to such an accusation. There is much indeed, however, to be found in the books and choice of friends of his son, Léon, to confirm the latter's militant anti-Semitism. From all that is known of Alphonse Daudet, it would have been completely contrary to his character for him to commit himself to any form of race discrimination or hatred. That such a label should have become attached to him would appear to be a case of the sins of the son being visited upon the father. Léon Daudet states in his *Memoirs* that his father, a couple of months before his death and then an ill and exhausted man, expressed his agreement with the military judges who had just convicted Dreyfus. And there are various reports that at a literary dinner Daudet attended a few days before his death the conversation turned to the Dreyfus case, and an argument developed between Zola, who favoured revision, and Daudet, who sided with the judges.

Daudet died a few days later at home, while at dinner with his family. For over fifteen years he had suffered pain so acute that it could only be relieved by constant drugs. Twelve years before his death, on the occasion of Victor Hugo's funeral in 1885, when asked to sign his name in the register, he had been unable to control the pen. In 1882, when his income from his books had reached what would today be about £12,000 a year,* he acquired the full-time services of his secretary, Jules Ebner, whose help he came to rely on increasingly and who was with him when he died. No part of his body was free from lightning attacks of pain. He never slept without chloral or injections of morphia. In 1887 his friend Charcot, the nerve specialist, diagnosed his illness as locomotor ataxy. Despite all his suffering he was never heard to complain. He believed firmly that all judgements are pronounced and all sentences served on earth. 'I believe absolutely in the formula of "everything must be paid for"; I have always seen man reap the wages of his toil, whether he toiled for good or evil, and not in the next life, which I do not know, but in this one, in ours, sooner or later.' (*La Lutte pour la vie.*)

All that can be brought, therefore, to substantiate any charge that Daudet was an anti-Semite is coloured by the testimony of those who were dealing, very shortly before he died, with a man who had been enduring a living death for many years. Against it can be set the fact that Theodor Herzl, the founder of political Zionism, placed on record†

*By 1890 his income was said to be about £40,000 a year in modern money.

†Leon Kellner, *Theodor Herzls Tagebücher*, Berlin, 1922–23, vol. 1, p. 14; *Theodor Herzl*, Berlin, 1920, p. 155.

that he owed to Alphonse Daudet vital encouragement, support and inspiration in the planning of his book *Der Judenstaat* (The Jewish State) which launched the Zionist movement and led eventually to the founding of the state of modern Israel. To say the least, this renders highly questionable the attempts of those who tried to label Daudet an anti-Semite.

Such then was the case against Daudet even in his lifetime, at the height of his reputation. Though not quite the equal of his friends Zola and Flaubert, he remains today a major figure in French literature, and it is more than time his best works were made available in the English-speaking world. If and when that should come about, there will be a place for a fuller examination of his life and achievement than can be given here. For the present purpose, a brief examination of his unique style in relation to his *Letters from my Windmill* may be helpful.

From the *Journals* of the Goncourt brothers and from accounts left by many of his friends, we know that Daudet possessed to an astonishing degree the natural ability to tell a story aloud. All witness to the spell-binding vividness, skill and charm of his conversation. Edmund Gosse, who met Daudet during his visit to London in 1895 on the occasion of a brief improvement in his health, wrote:

The entire physical aspect of Alphonse Daudet in these late years presented these contradictions. He would sit silent and almost motionless; suddenly his head, arms and chest would be vibrated with electrical movements, the long, white fingers would twitch in his beard, and then from the lips a tide of speech would pour – a flood of coloured words. On the occasion when I met him at dinner, I recollect that at dessert, after a long silence, he was suddenly moved to describe, quite briefly, the melon-harvest at Nîmes when he was a boy. It was an instance, no doubt, of the habitual magic of his style, sensual and pictorial at its best; in a moment we saw before us the masses of golden-yellow and crimson and sea-green fruit in the little market-place, with the incomparable light of a Provençal morning bathing it all in crystal. Every word seemed the freshest and the most inevitable that a man could possibly use in painting such a scene, and there was not a superfluous epithet.*

Daudet's brilliance as a conversationalist was widely and publicly acclaimed. He was not a born writer and does not appear to have suffered from that inner compulsion to write which is associated with Balzac, Simenon, Melville, Faulkner and others. By sheer hard work he forged a style which transmuted his great oral skill into the second of his two greatest assets as a writer: by many years of perseverance in journalism he acquired as a writer the skill with which as a speaker he could establish such a unique rapport with his listeners.

An examination of his style reveals he used a large number of devices to achieve this rapport. Daudet called his style *littérature debout*, 'standing-up literature', to suggest its close relationship with the spoken word. It is worth noting some of these devices.

His frequent interpolation of asides, from author to reader, have the same intention as when used by a speaker to cast a spell over his audience. So has his fondness for the informality of tone of first-person narrative: this became his favourite way of dispelling literary solemnity, of appearing to speak directly to his readers. He employs also the device of shifting the narrative from third-person to first-person and vice versa. The use of this device has more recently been brought as near perfection as it probably can be by Georges Simenon, though Simenon uses it chiefly and most effectively, as André Gide was one of the first to note, in order to tell a story in two and even three sequences of time. Daudet uses it to plunge the reader into the thoughts of his charac-

*Edmund Gosse, *French Profiles*, Heinemann, 1904, p. 120.

ters and to convey a more vivid sense of realism and immediacy. The reader will notice numerous instances of Daudet's use of this device in *Letters from my Windmill*.

Daudet, also, knew exactly what he was doing when he loosened the rigorous syntax and word-order of French sentences; his aim was to introduce the personal idiosyncrasies of conversation, to make the reader pleasantly aware of the 'persona' of the writer. Much of Daudet's so-called 'charm' is the result of the warmth and intimacy of his conversation transferred with great subtlety to the written word.

Again, Daudet's extensive use in this book of three dots ... is very noticeable. This, of course, is part of his technique of narrative impressionism. In order to spare the reader long, detailed passages of description and to give a feeling of pace, Daudet often uses an almost telegraphic prose which conveys an impression rather than a precise picture. By the omission of normal connectives and by the careful choice of adjectives and images arranged and juxtaposed with great skill, he compresses a complex wealth of meaning and feeling into a single sentence. His long, periodic sentences are interspersed with extended lists of images. He creates an almost pictorial rhythm of rhetoric by means of collages of sensual images, followed by a mounting series of periodic sentences which often have their own plastic rhythm of distance and closeness. A peak is reached and the reader is returned to the pictorial yet melodious rhythm of image piled on image.

Thus the beauty of Daudet's prose is both visual and musical: what Walter de la Mare called 'eye-music'. Daudet chooses and orders words as a poet does: for their sound, for their music. He chooses and orders his images as a painter does his colours: for their *impressioniste*, *pointillé* effect.

This style, so vivid and picturesque, often colloquial and confidential, often suggestive of meanings implied but never stated, makes Daudet difficult to translate. It was also much criticized. Even Anatole France censured him for lack of balance, for experimenting with constructions, for constantly using rare terms, for being almost too full of idiom. Yet, after finding as many faults as they can, most of his critics admit that his charm disarms criticism, and Anatole France ends his censure with: 'But does it all matter? Monsieur Daudet will always be right for me.'

What does not appear to have been noted by the critics is the debt Daudet obviously owed to Montaigne. The essays of Montaigne were Daudet's favourite books. He carried his Montaigne with him everywhere; reference to this will be found in *The Poet Mistral* in this book. It is very relevant therefore to remember that in his later essays Montaigne's prose style approximated more and more closely to the spoken word. Montaigne himself admitted that he passed from one subject to another, as in conversation, without the connecting words which are usually introduced. He cut up his sentences into short phrases, separated by full-stops and colons. He frequently indulged in the interpolations he so much admired in Plutarch. All these points have been noted with regard to Daudet's style. And, given Daudet's admiration for Plutarch's *Lives* (mentioned with obvious approval in *The Lighthouse of Les Sanguinaires*) as well as for Montaigne's *Essays*, it is evident that his deliberately cultivated style of *littérature debout* owed much to his reading of these two authors.

The letters in this book have already been alluded to incidentally in the foregoing pages. When it was published in book form *Letters from my Windmill* barely reached a sale of 2,000 copies, and, as Daudet mentions in his preface, only attained general popularity after the success of his novels. The subjects vary greatly in subject and mood, and it may come as a surprise to some readers to find that a number of these stories are tragic or at least grim. Only a few are humorous, and even in these the humour is nearly always ironic. But what they all have in common is the intimate tone of casual conversation with which they are told.

The main themes of all the books Daudet afterwards wrote are to be found in these early stories. The theme of Provence and its people, landscape, language and customs colours most of them, though a few are the result of his travels in Corsica and Algeria. The theme of artistic integrity with, to Daudet, its corollary: the destructive force latent in the artistic gift, is apparent in 'The Poet Mistral', 'Monsieur Seguin's Goat', 'Bixiou's Wallet', and 'The Fable of the Man with the Golden Brain'. Daudet became almost excessively concerned with this theme – in *Le Petit Chose, Les Femmes d'artistes, Jack, Sapho,* and in *L'Immortel.* He returned again and again to the idea that the gift of artistic genius is also a curse, a source of suffering to the gifted one and to all around him: a subject since examined brilliantly by Edmund Wilson in his *The Wound and the Bow.* The affinity of this theme with Strindberg is strangely complemented by Daudet's third theme in *Letters from my Windmill,* since it is one which became an obsession with Strindberg. This is Daudet's theme of love, of a man suffer-at the hands of a predatory, unscrupulous, but irresistible woman, and it appears in this volume in 'The Beaucaire Stage-coach', in 'The Girl from Arles' and in 'The Two Inns'. Noticeable in these three stories is that Daudet casts himself in the role of observer and so is able to shield himself from the involvement and pain which would result from writing them more personally in the first person. But it is his novel *Sapho* which reveals most deeply Daudet's understanding of the misery and jealousy which can result from bondage to such a woman. To Ernest Daudet, *Sapho* was always full of poignant memories of his brother's youth in Paris. And there can be no doubt that Daudet's view of love was always coloured by the happiness and pain of his long and passionate liaison with Marie Rieu, the artist's model, who occupied a room in the lodging-house in which he and his brother lived in Montmartre during their first years in Paris.

Finally, since no account of Daudet's life and achievement, however brief, would be complete without some mention of Daudet the man, here are two excerpts from the recollections of the only two intimate friends he made in England. Mrs Belloc Lowndes, sister of Hilaire Belloc, wrote:

At the time I first met Alphonse Daudet he was about fifty, and I repeat what was certainly true – he and Zola dominated the French literary scene, though Daudet, unlike Zola, shrank from any form of self-advertisement. Of the many French and English writers I have known well, Daudet remains in my memory as having possessed the most remarkable personality . . . We became friends from the first hour I spent with him in his plainly furnished study. He could not get up to greet a visitor and was always in pain. The strongly marked features of his pale face were surmounted by a shock of grey-black hair, and his body had become the wreck of a powerfully built man. He had a simple, kindly manner, and was an amazingly brilliant and varied talker. I never heard him even allude to any of his books. He was passionately interested in every sort of human creature, and was always willing to see, advise and encourage any young person who wished to write. I doubt if any man was ever kinder and more selfless with regard to those of his own craft than was Alphonse Daudet. He was the only well-known literary man or woman I have ever known who went on reading manuscripts sent him by unknown people, and telling them what he thought of their work. He remembered his own beginnings, and how two French writers of the day had sent him back his manuscript, saying they had had to make it a rule to refuse to look at any work submitted to them for an opinion. And were that the only thing to Daudet's credit, I think it proves him to have been, as was once said to me by Ebner, his devoted friend and secretary, a man of inexhaustible kindness of heart ... When I knew him, he had the same kind of bitter horror of poverty which Bernard Shaw, who possesses certain of Daudet's fine human qualities of kindness and compassion, once expressed ... He shared a belief I have long held: that life is a balanced ration; yet he is the only man who ever said to me, 'I am an absolutely happy man.'*

And his friend Robert Sherard tried to convey how the passionate young Provençal, with his captivatingly handsome looks and his ardent appetite for life, had been transformed into the tragic figure of thirty years later:

The hair is grey now, though still abundant. The eyes, save in moments of excitement, have lost much of their pristine fire; the warm amber of the complexion has faded, there is little purple left in the lips; pain has left its impress everywhere, like a fire it has scorched and seared and furrowed, and yet Alphonse Daudet's marvellous beauty remains.†

Kindness ... compassion ... beauty: they still remain, in his books; and in none more so than in his *Letters from my Windmill*.

*Mrs Belloc Lowndes, *Where Love and Friendship Dwelt*, Macmillan, 1943, p. 164.
†Robert H. Sherard, *Alphonse Daudet: A Biographical and Critical Study*, Edward Arnold, 1894.

TRANSLATOR'S NOTE AND ACKNOWLEDGEMENTS

THE editions of *Lettres de mon Moulin* which I possess and which I used in making this translation are:

1. Édition Définitive, Paris, Bibliothèque-Charpentier, 1913.
2. Nelson, Éditeurs, 189 rue Saint-Jacques, Paris. (Collection Nelson.)
3. Lausanne, Plaisir de Lire, 1958.

The last contains the Preface *Ce Que C'Était Que Mon Moulin* referred to in my Introduction and which I have not been able to find included in any other edition published since 1900. It was apparently first written as an article in 1883 and then included by Daudet as a Preface to *Lettres de mon Moulin* in the Collected Edition of his works.

It has been claimed that Daudet's prose style is untranslatable, and it is true he presents certain difficulties. He piles adjective upon adjective, detail upon detail, image upon image, juxtaposing impressions in often extremely long complex sentences. He is constantly using idiomatic and colloquial expressions. He occasionally uses words allusively; words which have a double meaning in French but not in English. He is forever experimenting with grammatical constructions.

Thus when one reads Daudet in the original one tends to feel the great charm and power of his style without perceiving that its apparent simplicity hides a most intricate craftsmanship. The translator's problem is to find an equivalent in English for this deceptively unobtrusive, highly idiosyncratic, richly allusive prose style and yet retain as much as possible of the unique charm and power of the original.

In my attempt to achieve this, I have had to alter and correct every page of my translation two, three or four times before feeling satisfied that the right word, phrase, balance, rhythm have been found. I wish therefore to thank Mr Colin Orsich for so patiently transcribing so many heavily altered and corrected drafts.

To Mrs Nell Green I owe the typing of a manuscript whose unusually varied punctuation demanded constant alertness.

And to Edward Ardizzone, (C.B.E.) I owe an immeasurable debt for illustrations which not only capture the spirit of Daudet's elusive charm but which are works of art in their own right.

F. D.

My Windmill as I First Knew It

ON the road that runs from Arles to the quarries of Font-vieille,* past the Mont de Corde and the Abbey of Montmajour, there rises above and a little to the right of a large village powdery-white as a stone-mason's yard, a small hill crowned with green pines – so green the sight of them almost quenches one's thirst in that sun-baked countryside. High up there, the sails of the windmills are forever turning; down below nestles a large white house, the manor-house of Mont***, a strange old dwelling which starts as a château with its flights of steps, its terrace colonnaded in the Italian style, and which finishes with farmhouse walls, perches for peacocks, vines over the door-way, a fig tree twining itself around the iron well-head, sheds glittering with harrows and ploughshares, a sheepfold next to a field of slender almond-trees whose pink blossoms are too quickly scattered by the winds of March. They are the only flowers at Mont***. No lawns or flowerbeds, nothing that recalls the garden, the well-tended estate; only clumps of pines among the grey of the rocks, a piece of enclosed land still in its wild natural state, its tangled, overgrown paths slippery with dry pine-needles. Inside, the same incongruity between château and farmhouse: cool, paved galleries,

*In all editions of *Lettres de mon Moulin* which I have been able to consult, 'Fontvieille' is spelt thus. The name of the actual place, how-ever, is spelt 'Fontvielle'. The former may have been an early printer's error since perpetuated, or it may have been a deliberate spelling of the word by Daudet as a thin disguise.

furnished with sofas and Louis XIV armchairs, cane-bottomed and shapely, so comfortable for summer siestas; wide staircases, stately corridors along which the wind rushes and whistles under the doors of the bedrooms, flickering the rush-lights of olden days. Then, down two steps, and behold the farmhouse kitchen, with its uneven floor of beaten earth in which the hens scratch for the crumbs from breakfast, with its rough-cast walls, its walnut sideboards, its artlessly carved bread-box and kneading-trough.

An old Provençal family lived there twenty years ago, not less unusual and charming than their dwelling. The mother, from a middle-class farming family, very old but still erect under the widow's bonnets she always wore, managed alone this considerable domain of olive groves, wheat-fields, vine-yards, mulberry plantations; with her, her four sons, old bachelors known by the professions they had followed or were still following; the Mayor, the Consul, the Notary and the Advocate. After the death of their father and the marriage of their sister, all four had rallied round the old woman, sacrificing for her all their hopes and ambitions, united in their exclusive love of her whom they called, always respectfully and yet always tenderly, their *chère maman*.

A house blessed by good people! . . . So many times, in winter, have I come there to seek the healing touch of Nature, to cure myself of Paris and its fevers in the health-giving air of the little hills of our Provence. I would arrive without warning, sure of the welcome proclaimed by the trumpet-calls of the peacocks and the barking of the three dogs, Miracle, Miraclet and Tabour who would keep leaping around my carriage, whilst the *arlésienne* head-dress of the startled maid wobbled as she ran to tell her masters, and whilst *chère maman* held me close to her little grey-checked shawl, as if I were one of her 'boys'. Five minutes of tumultuous excitement, then, the embracings over, my trunk in my room, all the house became once more silent and calm. I would whistle old Miracle – a spaniel found adrift at sea on a piece of wreckage by some Faraman fisherman – and I would climb up to my windmill.

A ruined windmill: a crumbling pile of stones and old wooden beams which had not turned in the wind for many years and which stood there helpless, as useless as a poet, while on the hillside all around, the milling trade was prospering and all the sails were turning.

Between ourselves and things strange affinities exist. From the first day I saw it, this abandoned outcast of a windmill had been dear to me; I loved it for its distressed condition, for its path lost under the herbs, those little, greyish, sweet-scented mountain herbs with which Father Gaucher mixed his elixir; I loved it for its crumbling platform where it was good to idle the hours away sheltered from the wind, while a rabbit bobbed up and down close by or a long grasssnake went its aloof and tortuous way as it pursued the field-mice which swarmed around the tumbledown mill. And when the mill's ramshackle walls creaked under the force of the *tramontane*, the noise of the rigging of its tattered sails stirred memories in my tired and anxious mind of sea-voyages, of halts at lighthouses, of far-off islands; and the sighing surge of the encircling pines completed the illusion. I do not know from where I have derived this liking for deserted and savage places. It has been with me since childhood and seems to accord so little with my natural exuberance. Perhaps it arises from a physical need to compensate, by an avoidance of speech, by an abstention from words and gesticulations, for the tremendous prodigality with which the southerner expends his whole being. Whatever the reason, I owe a great deal to such spiritual retreats; and none did me so much good as this old windmill in Provence. For a short while I even came near to buying it;

and possibly there can still be found in the office of the Notary at Fontvieille a deed of sale which remained a draft only but which has served me as the foreword of this book.

My windmill never belonged to me. That used never to prevent me from passing long days there, days of dreams and memories, until the hour when the winter sun would set between the little shaven hills filling their clefts as if with molten metal, a fuming flow of gold. Then, at the call of a marine conch, the horn of Monsieur Seguin calling home his goat, I used to return for the evening meal at the hospitable and fantastic table at Mont***, where each served himself according to his settled habits and tastes; the bottle of Constance wine for the Consul next to the *eau bouillie* or the plate of chestnuts of which the old mother made her frugal meal. Coffee over, pipes lit, the four bachelors gone off to the village, I would stay alone to talk with that excellent old lady, so good and so full of life, with her subtle mind, and her memory full of tales which she told with such simple eloquence: of her childhood, of human kindness no longer practised, of customs long vanished, of the vermilion on the leaves of the kermes-oak, of 1815, of the invasion and the great joy of all mothers at the fall of the Empire, of the dancing, the bonfires in the town squares, and the handsome Cossack officer, wearing the robe of a member of the French Academy who made her skip like a goat, dancing the farandole all night long on the bridge of Beaucaire. Then her marriage, the death of her husband, that of her eldest daughter, revealed to her when she was several leagues distance away by a presentiment, a sudden leap of her heart, of funerals and of births, of the moving of beloved ashes when the old cemetery was closed. It was as if I had turned the pages of one of those ancient family Bibles in which people once used to record the personal history of their families, all mixed up with ordinary details of their everyday life, the accounts of good wine years side by side with sheer miracles of self-sacrifice and submission to the will of God. In this middle-class but semi-rustic woman, I sensed a very feminine, sensitive, intuitive soul with the mischievous and uninstructed charm of a little girl. Weary of talking, she would sink back in her great armchair, some distance from the lamp; the shades of another falling night would close her sunken eyelids, invading her old, deeply lined face, wrinkled, cracked, furrowed deep by life's ploughshare and harrow; so silent, so motionless, I would have believed her to be sleeping, but for the click of her rosary, told by her fingers deep in her pocket. Then I would quietly go away to spend the rest of my evening in the kitchen.

Under the hood of a gigantic fireplace where the brass lamp would be hanging on its hook, a numerous company would be gathered in front of a bright fire of olive-roots whose spasmodic flames used to light up strangely the pointed head-dresses and the yellow woollen jackets. On the stone hearth, in the place of honour, squatted the shepherd, clean-shaven, sunburnt, his short pipe in the corner of his finely drawn mouth. He scarcely ever spoke, having acquired the habit of contemplative silence during the long months looking after his flocks high up on the Dauphiné Alps, close to the stars which he knew so well, from John of Milan to the Chariot of Souls.

Between puffs of his pipe, in his sonorous patois he would occasionally interject fragments of parables or some strange proverbs. I have kept some of them:

'*The man by his words and the ox by his horns . . . Monkeywork, little and badly . . . Pale moon, rain soon . . . Red moon, wind soon . . . Moon white, day bright.*' And every evening he would close the session with the same incongruous remark: '*The more the old woman got about, the more she learnt, and that's why she didn't want to die.*'

Near him, Mitifio the gamekeeper, nicknamed 'Pistolet',

with his laughing eyes and little white beard, used to amuse the company with numerous tales and fables, bringing out each time their saucy, scoffing side in a way very typical of Provence. Sometimes, in the midst of the laughter raised by one of Pistolet's stories, the shepherd would say, very seriously: 'If you are thought to be wise just because you have a white beard, goats ought to be as well.' There were also old Siblet, Dominique the coachman, and a little hunchback nicknamed 'The Prowler', a sort of hobgoblin and village spy, whose sharp eyes could pierce walls and the darkest night, a choleric soul, devoured by religious and political hatreds.

You should have heard him imitating and telling stories about Jean Coste, a revolutionary of 1793, dead not long since and faithful to his beliefs to the last. One of these told how Jean Coste travelled twenty leagues on foot just to see the priest and the two curates of his village guillotined. 'Ah, yes, my lads, it was when I saw them put their heads through the lunette of the guillotine – and it didn't suit them, passing their heads through the lunette – devil take me, it suited me all right . . . yes, lads, I got a lot of pleasure out of that . . .' Jean Coste, shivering all over, warming his old carcase against some sunlit wall and saying to the lads gathered round him: 'Well, young fellows, any of you ever read Volney? . . . Jouven, have you read Volney? That fellow proves by mathematics that the sun is the only God. I swear it! In the name of God! Only the sun!' And his judgements on the men of the Revolution: 'Marat, a good-hearted chap . . . Saint-Just, a good-hearted chap . . . Danton too, a good-hearted chap . . . Spoilt himself in the end though . . . Fell off and became a moderantist!' And the death-struggle of Jean Coste, stretched out like a ghost on his bed and speaking French for once in his life in order to hurl into the priest's face: 'Get out, you crow! . . . The carrion isn't dead yet!' With such terrible force would the hunchback repeat these last words, the women used to cry out: 'Oh, Holy Mother of God!' And the sleeping dogs would waken and leap, growling, towards the door against which the night wind was beating and moaning, until a woman's voice, clear and fresh, began to sing, to relieve the disturbed atmosphere, some Christmas song by Saboly: 'I saw in the air . . . an angel all in green . . . who had great wings . . . on his shoulders . . .' or, more likely, the arrival of the Wise Men in Bethlehem: 'Behold the King of the Moors – with his eyes all rolling sideways – the Child Jesus weeps – the King no longer dares to enter . . .,' a simple lively air for the three-holed flute of Provence, which I made a note of, together with all the impressions, turns of phrase, local traditions I gathered around the ashes of that ancient hearth.

Sometimes, too, my fancy would lead me roaming on little excursions around my windmill. It might be a shooting or a fishing trip to the Camargue, that pampas-like corner of Provence where the oxen and the wild horses are allowed to roam unfettered and free. Another day I would go and join my friends the Provençal poets, the Félibres. At that time the Félibre had not yet become established as an academic institution. We were still a small coterie, fervent and naïve, without schisms or rivalries. Five or six good friends, much given to poking fun at the literary establishment of the day, we would meet sometimes at Mallaine, Frédéric Mistral's little village, from which the Lower Alps separated me, sometimes in the Forum at Arles in the midst of a swarming mass of cattlemen and shepherds waiting to hire themselves out to the farmers. We used to go to the Céliscamps and, lying in the grass between the grey stone tombs, listen to some fine play by Théodore Aubanel, and the air all around us would be vibrating with the sound of the cicadas, ironically accompanied by the banging hammers of the railway workshops from behind a curtain of lustreless trees. After the reading we would stroll along the Lice to watch the proud, coquettish girls of Arles pass by under their wimples and their little white caps – for the love of one of whom poor Jan killed himself. At other times we would arrange to meet at the town of Les Baux, that dusty pile of ruins, sharp rocks, and old emblazoned palaces, crumbling, quivering in the wind like high eagles' nests from which can be discerned, beyond seeming endless plains, a line of pure, sparkling blue which is the sea. We would have supper at Cornille's inn and all the evening we would wander on, singing songs, through the little rambling side-streets, past crumbling walls, remains of flights of steps, broken columns, all shining with a ghostly brilliance so that the very grass and stones seemed overlaid with a light layer of snow. 'Poets . . .!' old Cornille used to say. 'Those people who love looking at ruins by moonlight.'

The Félibrige used also to meet among the reeds on the island of La Barthelasse opposite the ramparts of Avignon and the Palace of the Popes – which had witnessed the adventures and intrigues of little Tistet Védène. Then, after a lunch at some water-side tavern, we would go up to Château-Neuf-des-Papes, to the home of the poet Anselme Mathieu, famed for his vines, for long the most renowned in Provence. Ah, that wine of the Popes, that golden, royal, imperial, pontifical wine we used to drink high up on the hillside, chanting the poetry of Mistral, just-written pieces of 'The Golden Islands': 'In Arles, in olden magical times – there bloomed like a rose – the royal Queen Ponsirade . . .' or, perhaps the beautiful song of the sea: 'Cargo of oranges, sailing from Majorca . . .' And then we could indeed believe ourselves in Majorca, under its burning sky, surrounded by its sloping vineyards buttressed by low dry stone walls, among its olives, pomegranates and myrtles. Through the tavern's open windows, our verses took wing, and on the wings of our songs we also would be borne, for days at a time, across the joyous countryside of Comtat, rushing past fairs and bull-brandings, making short stops in the little towns under the plane trees of the gardens and squares, and, from our high seats on the charabancs that carried us, waving and shouting and distributing our nostrums to the assembled crowds. Our nostrums were simply Provençal verses, beautiful poetry in the language of those peasants, who understood and applauded the stanzas of *Mireille* by Mistral, of *The Venus of Arles* by Aubanel, of stories by Anselme Mathieu or Roumanville, and who joined with us in the chorus of the song of the sun: 'Glorious sun of Provence – gay companion of the Mistral – our wind which bubbles the Durance – like a glass of wine from Crau . . .' All would end with an improvised ball, a farandole, lads and lasses in working clothes and corks popping over the little tables. And if some old woman, a mumbler of prayers, happened to criticize our unrestrained gaiety, the handsome Mistral, regal as David the King, would look down at her and say: 'Enough, enough, mother . . . Poets are permitted to do what they will.' And then, winking confidentially at the old woman who would now be bending her head in respect, dazzled by his splendour, he would add: 'It is we who wrote the psalms . . .'

And how good it was, after one of these lyrical escapades, to come back to the windmill, to lie full-length on the grass on the platform, and dream of the book I would write one day, telling about it all, a book into which I would put all those songs, still singing in my head, all that bright laughter, all those enchanting legends; and in it I would reflect the light of that vibrant sun and the scent of those sun-parched hills, and I would write it as if it had been written in my ruin with its dead sails.

The first *Letters from my Windmill* appeared around 1866 in a Paris newspaper. Signed at first with a double pseudonym borrowed from Balzac, Marie-Gaston, these tales of Provence caused a sensation through their unusual theme. Gaston was my friend, Paul Arène, who, though still young, had just made his bow at the Odéon with a one-act play sparkling with wit and colour, and who lived near me at the edge of the wood at Meudon. But though this perfect writer did not yet have to his credit his *Jean des Figues* or his *Paris ingénu*, he already had too much talent, too positive a personality to be content for long with this work as assistant miller. So I was left to grind my little tales alone, at the caprice of the wind, the hour and the exigencies of a shockingly restless life. There were many times when I put them to one side; then I got married and I took my wife to Provence to show her my windmill. Nothing had changed there, neither the countryside nor the welcome. The old mother held us both tenderly against her little checked shawl and room was made at the 'boys'' table for the bride. My wife sat beside me on the platform of the windmill where the tramontane, seeing this Parisian enemy of sun and wind, amused himself by ruffling her dress, bowling her over, whirling her away like Chénier's young Tarentine. And it was after my return from this journey that, recaptured by my Provence, I began in *Figaro* a new series of the *Letters from my Windmill*: 'The Old Couple', 'The Pope's Mule', 'Father Gaucher's Elixir', etc., all written in that studio of Eugène Delacroix of which I have spoken in *Jack* and *Robert Helmont*. The book was published by Hetzel in 1869, and sold with difficulty 2,000 copies. It had to wait, like all my other early works, until the demand for my novels caused them to be known and so revived their sale. But that matters little now. It is still my favourite book, not from the literary point of view, but because it recalls for me the most splendid days of my youth, hours of foolish laughter, moments of ecstasy never regretted, and friendly faces and places I shall never more see again.

Today, Mont*** is deserted. *Chère maman* is dead, the old bachelors scattered, the wine of Château-Neuf consumed to the lees. Where would I look for Miracle and Miraclet, Siblet, Mitifio, the Prowler? If I went I should find nobody there any more. Only the pines, I am told, have grown much taller, and above the sparkling green swell of their topmost branches, restored, its sails renewed, like a ship afloat, my windmill turns in the sunshine, a poet holding his head high, a dreamer facing life again.

ALPHONSE DAUDET

APPEARING before Maître Honorat Grapazi, notary, residing at Pampérigouste:*

Gaspard Mitifio, husband of Vivette Cornille, farmer at the place known as Cigalières and there domiciled;

Who by these presents has sold and conveyed, under legal and factual guarantees, and exempt from all debts, lieus and mortgages,

To Alphonse Daudet, poet, domiciled in Paris, here present and hereto consenting,

A windmill, situated in the valley of the Rhône, in the very heart of Provence, on a hill wooded with pines and oaks; the said windmill being abandoned for more than twenty years and not in a condition for the grinding of corn, as shown by the wild vines, mosses, rosemary and other parasitic growths which have climbed to the ends of the sails;

Notwithstanding this, such as it is, with its great wheel broken, with grass growing between the bricks on its platform, the said Alphonse Daudet, declares that he finds the said windmill of service to, and able to meet, the requirements of his work as a poet, accepts it as his own risk and without any recourse against the seller in consequence of repairs that may have to be made to it.

This sale has taken place on payment of the agreed price, which the said Alphonse Daudet, poet, has placed and deposited on the desk in cash, which amount has been

---

*A fictitious but proverbial locality. 'Go to Pampérigouste!' the equivalent of 'Go to Jericho!' (See also page 93.)

immediately checked and taken up by the said Mitifio, all in the sight of the undersigned notaries and witnesses, and of which receipt is hereby acknowledged without prejudice.

I

Settling-In

I T is the rabbits who have been taken aback! They had seen the door of the mill closed for so long and grass invading the platform, that they had come to believe the race of millers extinct. And finding the place suited them, they had made it a sort of general headquarters, a centre of strategic operations, the mill of Jemappes* of the rabbits. Without a word of a lie, on the night of my arrival there was a score of them, sitting in a circle on the platform, warming their paws in the light of the moon. In the time it took to open a gable window, frrt! the whole platform was in flight, their little white backsides scurrying away, tails in air, into the bushes. I hope very much they will come back.

Someone else also very taken aback on seeing me is the tenant of the first floor, a sinister old owl with the head of a thinker, who has lived in the mill for more than twenty years. I found him erect and still on the driving shaft in the midst of plaster and broken tiles. He looked at me for a moment with his round eye, then, quite startled at not recognizing me, he began to go: 'Hou! Hou!' and to shake his grey, dusty wings laboriously — these thinkers, they never use a brush! But does that matter? Such as he is, with his blinking eyes and glum look, this silent tenant pleases me much better than any other, and I hasten to renew his lease.

*In 1792 the French defeated the Austrians at the small town of Jemappes in Belgium. The young Duke of Chartres, afterwards King Louis-Philippe, established his headquarters in the windmill of a neighbouring village. This 'mill of Jemappes' has since remained famous in French history.

He retains, as in the past, the whole upper storey of the mill with an entrance through the roof. For myself, I retain the lower storey, a small white-washed room, low and vaulted like a refectory in a monastery.

It is there that I am writing to you, my door wide open, the sun pouring in. In front of me, a wood of beautiful pines descends to the foot of the hill. In the far distance, the Lesser Alps raise their delicate crests. There is no sound. Only, sometimes near, sometimes far-away, the sound of a fife, a curlew in the lavender, mule-bells on the road . . . All the beauty of this Provençal countryside is born of the sun; it lives by light.

Why then should you wish me to regret Paris, your noisy, dirty Paris? It is so perfect here in my mill! the corner I have been looking for, a small, warm, sweet-scented corner, a thousand leagues from newspapers, cabs, fogs! . . . The lovely things all around me here! It is hardly a week since I settled in here, yet already I am brimful with impressions and memories! Just listen to this! Only yesterday evening I witnessed the return of the flocks to a farm at the foot of the hill and I swear to you that I would not have exchanged that sight for all the first nights you have had in Paris this week. Listen and judge for yourself.

In Provence, when the warm weather comes, it is the custom to take the flocks up to the Alps. Beasts and men spend five or six months high up there, under the open sky, knee-deep in the grass. Then, with the first chill of autumn, they come down again to the farms to browse on the little grey hills, scented with rosemary. Well, yesterday evening, the flocks were returning. The farm entrance had been waiting wide open since morning for them; the pens had been strewn thick with fresh straw. As time passed people kept saying, 'Now they're at Eyguières, now at Paradou.' Then, all at once, towards evening, a great shout is heard: 'There

they come!' and, far off in the distance, we see the flock approaching in a halo of dust. The very road itself seems to be on the march ... The old rams lead the way, fierce-looking, their horns piercing the dusty air; behind them moves the main body of the sheep, the ewes a little weary, with their young trotting in their footsteps; the mules, with their red pompoms, follow carrying the day-old lambs in baskets which rock like cradles; then the dogs, dripping with sweat, their tongues almost touching the ground, and the shepherds, two great rascals in their home-spun russet cloaks which reach to their heels like ecclesiastical vestments.

All of them file joyously past us and squeeze through the farm gateway, their feet pattering like a shower of rain ... Inside you should see the commotion. From high up on their perches, the big, tulle-crested, green-and-gold peacocks have recognized the arrivals and welcome them with tremendous trumpet-calls. The hens, asleep in the hen-house, awake with a start. All are up – pigeons, ducks, turkeys, guinea fowl. The farmyard seems to have gone mad; the hens talk of making a night of it! It is almost as if each sheep had brought back in its wool, along with the scent of the rough Alpine grass, a little of that keen mountain air which intoxicates you and sets your feet dancing.

In the midst of all this commotion the flock reaches its quarters. The way the sheep settle-in is a delight to behold. The old rams are visibly moved on seeing their mangers again. The lambs, the very small ones, those who have been born on the journey and have never seen the farm, gaze round in wonder. But most moving of all to see are the dogs, those wonderful sheep dogs, thinking only of their charges, oblivious of everything else in the farm. The watch-dog calls to them in vain from inside his kennel; in vain the brimming bucket at the well beckons to them; they will see nothing, hear nothing, until their charges are all safely housed, until the big bolt is pushed home in the little wicket-gate, and the shepherds are seated at table in the lower room. Only then do they consent to make for their kennel, and there, while lapping their bowl of soup, they tell their farm friends all they did high up on the mountain, that dark grim place where there are wolves and great purple foxgloves brimful with dew.

2

The Beaucaire Stage-coach

It was the day I came here. I had caught the Beaucaire stage-coach, an old ramshackle conveyance which hasn't a long way to go before it finds its final home, but which dawdles along the roads in order to look as if it has come a long distance when it arrives in the evening. There were five of us on the outside, not counting the driver.

First, a man from the Camargue, squat, hairy, smelling of the world, with large bloodshot eyes and silver rings in his ears. Then two men from Beaucaire, a baker and his journeyman, both very red-faced, very wheezy, but with superb profiles, two Roman medallions with the head of Vitellius. Lastly, in front near the driver, a man ... no! a cap, an enormous, rabbit-skin cap which said little and looked sadly at the road.

All those people knew each other and kept talking about their affairs very loudly, and very freely. The man from the Camargue related how he was coming from Nîmes on a summons from the examining magistrate for having stabbed a shepherd with a pitchfork. They are hot-blooded in the Camargue ... And at Beaucaire it seemed! Weren't our two citizens of Beaucaire wanting to cut each other's throat on account of the Virgin Mary? It seemed that the baker was from a parish long devoted to the Madonna, whom the people of Provence call *la bonne mère* and who carries the little Jesus in her arms; the journeyman, on the other hand, sang bass in the choir of a quite new church consecrated to the Immaculate Conception, that beautiful smiling image which is represented with outstretched arms, and hands emitting rays of light. The quarrel arose over that. You would have had to see it to believe the way these two good Catholics behaved to each other and to their Madonnas:

'Immaculate! She's a fine one for you to call immaculate!'

'What about you and your good mother!'

'Yours got more than she bargained for in Palestine all right!'

'And yours! The naughty girl! Who knows what she didn't get up to . . . You'd better ask Joseph.'

One needed but to see the flash of knives to believe oneself on the harbour at Naples, and, by heavens, I do believe that's how this fine theological foray would have ended if the driver had not intervened.

'That's enough of your madonnas,' he said, laughing, to the men from Beaucaire. 'Leave that nonsense to the women folk. Men should keep out of it.'

Upon which, he cracked his whip in a slightly sceptical way, which made everybody accept his opinion.

The argument had ended, but having got going the baker had to get rid of his surplus energy, and turning to the miserable cap, silent and sad in his corner, said mockingly to him:

'That wife of yours, knife-grinder? Which parish receives her favours?'

There must have been something funny in this, the way everybody roared with laughter . . . Except the knife-grinder. He didn't appear to have heard. Seeing this, the baker turned to me:

'You don't know his wife, monsieur? Some wife she is, all right! There aren't two like her in Beaucaire.'

The laughter was twice as loud. The knife-grinder did not move. He merely said, very quietly without lifting his head:

'Shut up, baker!'

But that devil of a baker had no wish to shut up; he went on worse than ever:

'Fool! Any fellow with a wife like that has no call to feel sorry for himself! Never a boring moment with her about ... A beauty who goes off with somebody every six months, she's always plenty to tell you when she gets back ... All the same, it's a strange way to keep a marriage going ... Just think, monsieur, they hadn't been married a year and the wife is off to Spain with a fellow selling chocolate.

'The husband is left alone at home weeping and drinking ... He's like a madman. After a while, her ladyship is back again, decked out in a Spanish dress, with a little drum with bells on it. We all told her:

' "Hide yourself! He'll kill you!"

'Kill her! That was good! ... They settled down together again like two little doves and she taught him to play the drum.'

There was another roar of laughter. In his corner, without lifting his head, the knife-grinder murmured again:

'Shut up, baker!'

The baker took no notice and went on:

'Maybe you'll be thinking, monsieur, that when she got back from Spain, her ladyship took things quietly ... Not on your life! ... Her husband had taken it all so well! It made her want to try again ... After the Spaniard, it was an officer, then a sailor, then a musician, then a ... I can't remember them all. The joke is, each time it's the same old story. The wife goes off, the husband weeps. She comes back, he's himself again. She's always running off, and he's always taking her back. You must admit a husband like that has patience! Still, you have to take into account she's a real beauty, our little wife of a knife-grinder ... good enough for a cardinal: full of life, attractive, well-shaped; a white skin as well, and nut-brown eyes always giving the men laughing looks . . . Yes, by heavens, if you ever pass through Beaucaire again, my fine Parisian . . .'

'Oh, shut up, please, baker!' came again from the knife-grinder, a heart-rending note in his voice.

At that moment, the coach stopped. We were at the farm of Les Anglores. It was here the two men from Beaucaire got off, and I assure you I didn't try to detain them . . . Yes, he enjoyed teasing people, that baker! We could hear him still laughing when he was inside the farmyard.

With those two gone, the outside of the coach seemed empty. We had left the man from the Camargue at Arles; the driver was walking on the road beside his horses . . . We were alone up there, the knife-grinder and I, each of us in his corner, neither of us speaking. It was hot; the leather of the hood was too hot to touch. Now and then I felt my eyes close and my head became heavy; but sleep was impossible. I could still hear that 'Shut up, please', so woe-begone, so subdued . . . Nor was he sleeping, poor fellow! From behind, I could see his big shoulders shuddering, and his hand – a long, pale, simpleton's hand – trembling on the back of the seat, like an old man's hand. He was crying . . .

'Here you are, Parisian! You're there!' the driver shouted up suddenly at me; and with the end of his whip he showed me my green hill with the mill perched on top like a big butterfly.

I hurried to get down. As I passed close to the knife-grinder I tried to glance under his cap; I would have liked to see him before leaving. As if he understood my thoughts, the poor fellow flung up his head and looked me straight in the eyes:

'Take a good look at me, friend,' he said, in a toneless voice, 'and if one of these days you hear there has been a murder at Beaucaire, you will be able to say you've met the man who did it.'

He had a wan, sad face, with little shrunken eyes. There were tears in those eyes, but in that voice there was hate. Hate – that is what becomes of the anger of weak men . . . If I were that knife-grinder's wife, I should be on my guard.

3

Old Cornille's Secret

An old fife-player, Francet Mamäi, who comes now and then to drink a glass of mulled wine with me, told me the story the other evening of a little village drama which took place at my windmill some twenty years ago. I was moved by his tale, and I will try and retell it to you just as I heard it.

Imagine, for a moment, dear readers, that you are sitting with a pot of spiced wine before you, and that it is an old fife-player who is talking to you.

Our country, monsieur, has not always been the dead and songless place it is today. In former days the flour trade flourished here and the farmers for ten leagues around used to bring us their wheat to grind . . . The hills all about the village were dotted with windmills. Whichever way you looked, you could see sails turning in the mistral above the pines, and long strings of little donkeys laden with sacks going up and down the paths; and all week long it was a joy to hear on these hill-tops the cracking of whips, the creaking of the canvas of the sails, and the shouts of the millers' men. On Sundays, parties of us would climb up to the windmills and the millers would stand us all a glass of muscatel. The millers' wives were dressed like queens with their lace fichus and gold crosses. I would always bring my fife and they all used to dance the farandole* far into the night. These windmills, you see, were not only the wealth of our land, they were its pride and joy.

*A Provençal country dance; Daudet gives an extraordinarily vivid description of this dance at the beginning of his novel *Numa Roumestan*.

Unfortunately some Frenchmen from Paris had the idea of setting-up a steam-driven flour-mill on the road to Tarascon. As the saying goes, everybody has a penny to spend at a new ale-house and people began to get into the habit of sending their wheat to these fine new flour-mills, and soon there was no work left for the poor windmills. For a time they tried to make a fight of it, but steam-power was too much for them, and – alas and alack! – one after another they were all forced to close. The little donkeys were seen no more. The fine millers' wives sold their gold crosses. No more muscatel! No more farandoles! The mistral could blow its hardest, the sails remained motionless . . . Then, one fine day, the local government officials had all these ruined windmills pulled down and vines and olive trees were planted where they had stood.

Yet, in the midst of this catastrophe, one windmill held out and kept on bravely turning its sails despite all the steam-driven flour-mills. It was the mill of old Cornille, the same one in which, at this very moment, we are spending such a friendly evening.

Old Cornille was a miller who had practised his craft for sixty years, an achievement of which he was more than proud. The intrusion of the flour-mills maddened him to a state of fury. For a week he was to be seen running about the village seeking support, bellowing accusations that their aim was to poison all Provence with the flour from their steam-driven mills. 'Don't go near them,' he would say. 'Those thieves are using steam to make bread. It's an invention of the devil. I use the mistral and the tramontane, good winds invented by God . . .' And he would sing the praises of the windmills, but no one listened to him.

Then, in a fury, the old man shut himself up in his windmill and lived all alone like a wild beast. He would not even let his little granddaughter remain with him – a young girl, only fifteen, named Vivette, whose parents were dead and who had no one else in the world except her grandfather. The poor child had to earn her own living, working on farms, harvesting, silkworm picking, or olive-gathering. And yet her grandfather appeared to love the child very much. He often seemed to find himself walking four leagues in the heat of the day to see her at the farm where she was working. And when he was with her, he would gaze at her for hours at a time, weeping.

Everybody thought the old miller had sent Vivette away to avoid the cost of keeping her; and it did him no good in their eyes to allow his granddaughter to wander from one farm to another exposed to the coarse jokes of the shepherds and to all the misery endured by young girls in service. People, also, thought it disgraceful that a well-known man like old Cornille, who had always kept his self-respect, should be going about the streets like a complete vagabond, barefooted, holes in his cap, his waistband in rags ... Indeed, when we older people used to see him coming into Mass on Sundays, we used to feel ashamed for him; and Cornille realized this so much he no longer dared come and sit in the churchwarden's pew. He always remained at the back of the church, near the holy water, with the beggars.

There was one thing, though, about old Cornille that puzzled many people. For a long time nobody in the village had taken him any corn, yet the sails of his windmill kept turning as in the old days ... In the evenings we would meet the old man on the paths, driving his donkey laden with big sacks of flour before him.

'Good evening, Cornille,' the peasants would shout. 'The mill's still working, is it?'

'Never stops, my lads,' the old man would reply cheerfully. 'We don't lack for work, thanks be to God.'

But then, if anyone asked him where the devil he got so much work from, he would put his finger to his lips and answer solemnly: 'Keep it quiet! I'm working for the export trade . . .' Nobody could squeeze a thing more out of him.

As for putting your nose inside his mill, it was useless to think of it. Not even little Vivette could get in there . . .

Whenever you passed by his mill, you would see the door closed, the great sails always moving, the old donkey grazing on the platform, and a big, lean cat lying in the sun on the window-ledge giving you an evil look.

There was something mysterious about all this and it set people's tongues wagging. Everyone had his own theory about old Cornille's secret, but the general opinion was there were more bags of money in that windmill than there were sacks of flour.

However, everything was discovered in the end; here is how it all came out:

One fine day, whilst the young people were dancing to my fife, I discovered that my eldest boy and little Vivette had fallen in love with each other. All in all, I was not too displeased, because after all the name of Cornille was greatly respected in the district; and, besides, it would be a delight to me to see that pretty little Vivette trotting about the house. Moreover, as the two of them often had the chance of being together, I decided to settle the business at once, in case of accidents. So I went up the hill to have a word with the grandfather. You should have seen the welcome I got from the old devil! He wouldn't even open his door. I explained my business as well as I could through the key-hole, with that skinny villain of a cat spitting at me like a fiend above my head.

The old man didn't give me time to finish; he shouted at me in the most rude way to get back to my flute, and to go and find one of the girls from the flour-mills if I was in a hurry to get my son married. You can imagine how my blood boiled to be spoken to like that; but I had sense enough to control myself, and, leaving the old fool to his millstones, I went home and told the children how I had been treated . . . The poor innocents couldn't believe it possible. They begged me to let them go up to the mill and speak to him themselves . . . I hadn't the heart to refuse, and off they went as fast as they could.

When they got up there, old Cornille had just gone out. The door was double-locked, but the old fellow had left his ladder outside, which immediately gave the youngsters the idea of getting in by the window to see what was inside this mill everybody was talking about.

The mystery deepened! The grinding room was empty . . . Not one sack, not one grain of corn; not the faintest sign of flour on the walls nor on the cobwebs . . . There wasn't even the good warm smell of crushed wheat that fills all windmills like a perfume. The main shaft was covered with dust, and the big, lean cat was lying asleep on it.

The downstairs room had the same neglected, abandoned look: an unmade bed, a few rags, a piece of a loaf on one of the steps of the stairs, and then, there, in one corner three or four sacks which had burst open, spilling out broken plaster and other rubbish from pulled-down windmills.

So that was old Cornille's secret! It was this debris of plaster, bricks and mortar that he had been promenading up and down the paths every evening – to save the honour of his mill and make people think it was still grinding wheat and producing flour . . . Poor old Cornille and his mill! The flour-mills had robbed them of their last customer long ago. The sails had kept turning, but the millstones had had nothing to grind.

The two young people came back in tears and told me what they had seen. I had a feeling of deep sorrow as I listened to them . . . Without losing a moment I ran to my neighbours, quickly told them the facts and immediately it was agreed we must set off at once to Cornille's mill with all the wheat we could muster ... And that's what we did. The whole village set out and we arrived at the top of the hill with a procession of donkeys laden, with corn – with real corn, this time.

The mill door stood wide open! In front of it, seated on a bag of plaster, was old Cornille, with his head in his hands, weeping. He had just returned and, finding someone had entered the mill whilst he was away, had realized that his sad secret was his no longer.

'Woe is me!' he was saying. 'Now there's nothing to do but die ... I have brought shame on my mill.'

And he sobbed as though his heart were breaking, calling his windmill all sorts of pet names, speaking to it as if it were a real person.

It is then that the donkeys arrive on the platform and we all begin to shout at the top of our voices, just as we used to in the good old days:

'Hello, there, in the mill! Ho, there, Master Cornille!'

And now the sacks are piling up in front of the door, and all around the golden-brown corn is overflowing on to the ground ...

Old Cornille stared, his eyes wide. He had picked up some of the corn and, holding it in the palm of his hand, he was saying, over and over again, half-laughing and half-weeping:

'It's corn! ... Dear Lord in Heaven! ... Real corn! ... Let me look at it!'

Then, turning towards us:

'Ah! I knew so well you would come back to me! Those flour-millers with their steam engines – they are all a lot of thieves!'

We wanted to carry him on our shoulders in triumph to the village.

'No, no, my lads; before anything else, I must go and

give my mill something to eat . . . Just think! It hasn't been able to get its teeth into anything for such a long time!'

And it brought tears to our eyes to see the poor old man bustling about, slitting open the sacks, keeping an eye on the millstone, as it crushed the corn and sent the fine dust from the wheat rising to the ceiling.

In fairness to ourselves you must allow us this; from that day forward we never let the old miller want for work. But then, one morning, old Cornille died, and the sails of our last windmill stopped turning, for ever this time. Cornille dead, no one took his place. What can you expect, monsieur? Everything comes to an end in this world, and we shall have to get used to the idea that the windmills are things of the past, like the boats pulled by horses up the Rhône, and our local courts of justice, and the long tailcoats with flowers embroidered on them that the men used to wear.

4

Monsieur Seguin's Goat

To Monsieur Pierre Gringoire,
Lyrical Poet,
Paris.

You'll always stay in the same old rut, my poor Gringoire!*

Heavens above, man! You're offered a job on a good Paris news-sheet and you have the nerve to turn it down . . . Take a look at yourself, you poor wretch! Look at the holes in your doublet, the rents in your hose, and that thin face of yours with hunger written all over it. That's what ten years

*In Victor Hugo's *Notre-Dame de Paris*, Gringoire, who actually lived at the beginning of the sixteenth century, is represented as a penniless poet of the time of Louis XI. Hence Gringoire has come to be used as the typical name of such a character.

of writing poetry have done for you. Can't you bring yourself to admit you're ashamed of yourself?

Go and write for the news-sheets, you idiot! Become a chronicler, not a poet! You'd earn plenty of rose-nobles, you'd have your place reserved at Brébant's, and you'd be able to appear at first nights with a feather in your cap . . .

No? You'd rather not? You regard it as your right to remain free to do as you please, come what may? Very well, give ear a moment to the story of *Monsieur Seguin's goat*. That will show you what is to be gained by wanting to remain free.

Monsieur Seguin had always been unlucky with his goats.

He kept on losing them, and all in the same way: one fine morning they would break loose from their rope, go off up into the mountains, and be eaten by the wolf. Nothing – neither the caresses of their master nor fear of the wolf – could hold them back. They were, it seemed, independent goats, determined to have fresh air and freedom at any cost.

The good Monsieur Seguin, failing to appreciate this characteristic of his goats, was filled with consternation. He kept saying:

'It's no use. The goats get bored staying with me. I'll never manage to keep one.'

However, he did not give up, and, after having lost six goats in the same manner, he bought a seventh, but this time he was careful to find quite a young one, so that she might the better get used to living with him.

Ah, Gringoire, what a charming creature she was, that little goat of Monsieur Seguin's! How sweet she was with her gentle eyes, her little goatee beard, her black shining hoofs, and her long white coat that kept her as warm as a coachman's greatcoat.

She was nearly as charming as Esmeralda's* little goat – you remember, Gringoire? – and docile, too, affectionate, never moving while she was being milked, never putting her hoof in the milking pail. A pearl of a little goat . . .

Behind his house Monsieur Seguin had a field surrounded by a hawthorn hedge. Here he put the new lodger. He tied her to a stake in the most beautiful part of the meadow, taking care to allow her plenty of rope, and every now and then he came out to see if she was all right. The goat was very happy and ate the grass so heartily that Monsieur Seguin was delighted.

'At last,' thought the poor man, 'I've found one that won't get bored being with me!'

Monsier Seguin was mistaken. His goat got bored.

One day, looking up at the mountains she said to herself: 'How nice it must be up there! What fun to frolic about in the heather without this blasted rope scraping my neck! It's all right for a donkey or an ox to chew grass shut up in a field. Goats need plenty of room.'

From that moment all the grass in her field seemed tasteless. She became bored. She got thin and her milk fell off. It was pitiful to see her pulling at her rope all day, with her head turned towards the mountains, her nostrils wide open, bleating . . . sadly.

Monsieur Seguin saw very well something was wrong, but he couldn't make out what . . . Then one morning, just as he was finishing milking her, the goat turned round and said to him in dialect:

'Listen, Monsieur Seguin, I'm simply wasting away staying here with you. Let me go off to the mountains.'

*The gipsy girl in Hugo's *Notre-Dame de Paris* who is always accompanied by a little white goat. In the novel she saves Gringoire's life by offering to marry him, and Gringoire rescues the goat when she is burnt.

'Oh, good heavens! Now this one's at it!' exclaimed Monsieur Seguin in astonishment, getting such a shock he dropped the pail. Then, seating himself beside his goat, he said:

'Oh, Blanquette! You want to leave me?'

And Blanquette replied:

'Yes, Monsieur Seguin.'

'But haven't you enough grass here?'

'Oh, it's not that, Monsieur Seguin!'

'Is your rope too short? Would you like me to lengthen it?'

'It's not worth the trouble, Monsieur Seguin.'

'Then what's wrong? What is it you want?'

'I just want to go to the mountains, Monsieur Seguin.'

'But, you silly goat, don't you know the wolf is up there? Suppose you met him. What would you do then?'

'I'd butt him with my horns, Monsieur Seguin.'

'A lot the wolf cares for your horns! He's eaten goats of mine with far stronger horns than yours. Think of poor old Renaude, only last year – she was a nanny-goat who was as strong and vicious as any billy-goat – and she fought the wolf the whole night through . . . then, in the morning, the wolf ate her.'

'Alas! Poor Renaude! All the same, do let me go to the mountains, Monsieur Seguin.'

'Dear Lord!' exclaimed Monsieur Seguin. 'What is it gets into my goats? Here's another one the wolf's going to have a meal of at my expense. I won't stand for it! You silly nanny-goat, I'll save you in spite of yourself! I won't give you the chance to break your rope. I'll shut you up in the shed, and there you'll stay – for good!'

Thereupon, Monsieur Seguin carried his goat into a pitch-dark shed and double-locked the door. Unfortunately, he forgot the window, and as soon as he'd turned his back, the little goat was away . . .

You laugh, Gringoire? By heavens, I should have known you would! You're on the side of the goats against that kind Monsieur Seguin . . . Well, we'll see if you're still laughing in a moment.

When the little white goat reached the mountain everyone was delighted. The old fir trees had never seen anything so pretty. She was received like a princess. The chestnut-trees stooped low to caress her with the tips of their branches. The golden broom opened up a passage for her, and smelt as sweet as it could. The whole mountain welcomed her.

You can well imagine, Gringoire, how happy our little goat was! No more rope, no more stake, nothing to stop her frisking about and grazing where she could. The grass up there! My dear Gringoire, it reached up to her horns! And what grass! Of all varieties, tasty, delicate, fine as lace, all so very different from the grass in that enclosed field! The flowers, as well! Great blue hare-bells, long-cupped purple foxgloves, an entire forest of wild flowers, overflowing with luscious juices!

Half-drunk with it all, the little white goat kept throwing herself on her back and rolling down the slopes, scattering all around her the fallen leaves and chestnuts. Then, all at once, with a quick leap, she would be on her feet again. And away she would go, nose in the air, off among the shrubs and the maquis, now on a crag, now deep in a ravine, up, down, everywhere. You'd have thought that there were a dozen of Monsieur Seguin's goats on the mountain.

It was simply that little Blanquette was afraid of nothing!

With one flying leap, she would bound across great torrents which drenched her with their spray and foam. Then, soaking wet, she would stretch herself out on some rocky ledge and let the sun dry her. Once, coming to the edge of a plateau, she saw on the plain far, far below her,

Monsieur Seguin's house, with the field behind it. She laughed so much, the tears came into her eyes.

'What a tiny, little place!' she said. 'How did I ever put up with it?'

Poor little thing! Being so high up, she thought she had grown bigger, as big almost as the world itself.

To cut a long story short, Monsieur Seguin's goat spent a wonderful day. Towards noon, still running hither and thither, she came across a herd of chamois, enjoying a munching meal of wild vine. Our little white wanderer made quite a sensation. Room was made for her where the vines were best and all the gentlemen were most attentive. It would even appear – and this is between ourselves, Gringoire – that a young, black-haired chamois had the good fortune to please Blanquette. The two lovers lost their way in the wood for an hour or two, and if you would like to know what they said to each other you must ask those babbling brooks that wander unseen through the mosses.

Suddenly, the wind freshened. The mountain became purple-hued; evening had come.

'So soon!' said the little goat; and she stood still, quite astonished.

Down below, the fields were covered with mist. Monsieur Seguin's meadow was disappearing from sight and all that could be seen of his house was the roof with a little smoke rising from its chimney. She listened to the bells of a flock of sheep on their way home and she was overcome by a feeling of sadness ... A gerfalcon, returning home to its nest, touched her with its wing as it flew past. She jumped with fright ... Then a howling sound was heard on the mountain:

'Hoo! Hoooo!'

She thought of the wolf; all day long the silly creature hadn't given him a thought ... At the same moment a horn sounded far away below in the valley. It was the kind Monsieur Seguin making one last attempt.

'Hoo! Hoooo!' howled the wolf.

'Come back! Come back!' cried the horn.

Blanquette felt a sudden desire to go back; but then she remembered the stake, the rope, the hedge-enclosed field, and she thought that now she could never accept that life again, and that it would be better to stay.

The horn no longer sounded.

The goat heard a rustling of leaves behind her. She turned and saw in the darkness two short straight ears, and two shining eyes . . . It was the wolf.

Enormous, motionless, there he sat looking at the little white goat, tasting her already in his mind. Since he knew quite well he was going to eat her, the wolf was in no hurry; only when she turned and looked at him, did he begin to laugh wickedly.

'Ah, ha! If it isn't Monsieur Seguin's little goat!' And he licked his slavering chops with his huge, red tongue.

Blanquette felt she was lost . . . She remembered the story of old Renaude, who had fought all night long only to be eaten in the morning, and the thought passed quickly through her mind that perhaps it would be best to let herself be eaten at once. Then, changing her mind, she fell on guard, head down and horns forward, as any goat worthy of Monsieur Seguin would do. Not that she had any hope of killing the wolf – goats do not kill a wolf – but only to see if she would be able to hold out as long as Renaude had done . . .

Then the monster advanced, and the little horns attacked.

Oh, how courageously she stood her ground, that fine little goat! More than a dozen times – without a word of a lie, Gringoire – she forced the wolf to retreat to get his breath. During these short intervals, the little goat would greedily snatch a hasty bite of her beloved grass; then, her mouth full, she would return to the fight ... It lasted the whole night long. Every now and then, Monsieur Seguin's goat would look at the stars dancing in the cloudless sky, and say to herself:

'Oh, if I can only hold out until the dawn! ...'

One after another the stars went out. Blanquette's horns attacked fiercer than ever, the wolf's teeth sank deeper and deeper ... A pale light appeared along the horizon ... Down on a farm a cock crowed stridently ...

'At last!' said the poor animal, who had been awaiting the coming of day only so that she might die. And she laid herself down full length on the ground, her lovely white coat all stained with her blood ...

Then the wolf hurled himself on the little goat and ate her.

Goodbye, Gringoire!

I have not made up this story. If ever you come to Provence, our farmers will talk to you often about 'Monsieur Seguin's goat who fought the wolf the whole night through, and how then in the morning the wolf ate her'.

Hear well these words, Gringoire:

'... then in the morning the wolf ate her.'

5

The Stars

A PROVENÇAL SHEPHERD'S TALE

IN the days when I used to look after the sheep on the Luberon, I would go entire weeks without seeing a living soul, all alone up on the pastures with my dog, Labri, and my flocks. Now and then, the hermit from Mont-de-l'Ure used to pass by looking for herbs, or sometimes I would see the black face of some charcoal-burner from Piedmont; but these were simple folk, made silent by solitude, having lost the inclination to speak, and knowing nothing of what was being talked about down below in the villages and towns. So, every fortnight, when I used to hear coming up the mountain path the sound of the bells of the mule from our farm bringing me my fortnightly provisions, and when I would see the cheerful face of the little farm lad or the russet cap of old Aunt Norade appearing over the brow of the hill, I was indeed the happiest of men. I used to get them to tell me the news of the valley, the baptisms, the marriages; but what interested me most of all was to hear all that they could tell me about my master's daughter, Stéphanette, the prettiest girl for more than ten leagues around. Without appearing to be taking too much interest, I would find out whether she had been going to many fairs or dances, or whether new suitors were calling on her; and to those who may ask what that had to do with me, a poor mountain shepherd, my answer is that I was twenty years old and Stéphanette was the most beautiful girl I had seen in all my life.

But one Sunday it happened that the fortnightly provisions were late arriving. During the morning I had kept saying to myself: 'It's because of High Mass'; then, about midday, there was a violent storm and I thought perhaps the mule had not been able to set out owing to the bad state of the roads. At last, about three o'clock, the sky having cleared and the mountain shining with water in the sun, I heard above the dripping of the leaves and the bubbling of the waters of the swollen streams, the sound of the mule-bells, as clear and gay as a full peal of church bells on an Easter day. But it was not the farm boy, nor old Aunt Norade, who was leading the mule. It was . . . guess who? . . . my master's daughter Stéphanette in person, seated erect on the mule between the wicker panniers, her face pink and fresh from the mountain air and the storm.

The boy was sick, Aunt Norade on holiday with her children. Beautiful Stéphanette told me all this while getting off the mule, adding that she was late because she had lost her way; but to see her dressed in her best clothes, with her flowered ribbon, her laces, and her brilliantly glossy skirt, it seemed as if some dance had delayed her rather than the bushes through which she had had to find her way. Oh, what a daintily beautiful sight she was! I could not take my eyes off her. It is true I had never before seen her so close to. Sometimes, in winter, after the flocks had descended to the plain and I came into the farmhouse in the evening for supper, she would pass quickly through the room, hardly ever speaking to the servants, always beautifully dressed and a little proud . . . And now I had her there in front of me, just her and myself; was it not enough to turn my head?

When she had taken the provisions out of the panniers, Stéphanette began to look around her curiously. Lifting up her best skirt a little, to prevent it becoming soiled, she went into the sheepfold wishing to see the corner where I slept, the bedding of straw with its sheep skin, my great cloak hanging on the wall, my crook, my flintlock gun. It all gave her great amusement.

'So this is where you live, my poor shepherd? How bored you must be on your own all the time! What do you do? What d'you think about?'

I wanted to say: 'I think of you, mistress', and it would have been no lie; but I was so embarrassed I could hardly utter a word. I do believe she realized this and took a mischievous pleasure in increasing my embarrassment by saying:

'And does your sweetheart come up to see you sometimes, shepherd? I expect she must be the Fairy Estérelle who can only be seen on the mountain tops . . .'

And as she said this, she herself might have been the Fairy Estérelle, her head tilted back as she laughed so prettily, and her haste to be gone making her seem all the more a visitor from faeryland.

'Good-bye, shepherd.'

'Fare well, mistress.'

And she was gone, taking with her the empty baskets.

When she disappeared down the steep path, it seemed to me that the pebbles rolling from under the mule's hoofs were falling one by one on to my heart. I listened to them for a long, long time; and until the day was ending I remained as in a sleep, not daring to move for fear my dream should fade. Towards evening, as the deep valleys far below began to turn blue, and the sheep were all bunched together bleating to get back into the fold, I heard somebody calling to me from down the slope, and I saw my young mistress, no longer laughing as she had been only a short time before, but all wet and shivering with fear and cold.

It seemed that at the bottom of the slope she had found the waters of the Sorgue swollen after the storm, and in trying to cross she had nearly drowned. What made things all the worse was that it was out of the question to think of returning to the farm at that late hour because my mistress would never have been able to find the short-cut down the mountain all by herself, and it was impossible for me to leave my flock. The thought of having to spend the night on the mountain caused her great distress, mostly because her family would become anxious about her. I tried to reassure her as well as I could:

'The nights are short in July, mistress. They will only have a bad moment or two.'

And I quickly lit a big fire to dry her feet and her dress, dripping wet from the water of the Sorgue. Then I put some milk and cheese before her, but the poor girl could think neither of warming herself nor of eating, and when I saw great tears filling her eyes, I felt like weeping myself.

Meantime, night had come swiftly. On the misty mountain top facing the setting sun there remained only a rose-pink flush. I invited my young mistress into the sheepfold to rest there. After spreading out a fine new skin on top of some fresh straw, I wished her good night and sat down outside the door. God is my witness that in spite of the fire of love that was burning in my veins, no bad thought came to me, only a feeling of great pride that, in a corner of the sheepfold close to the sheep watching her curiously, my master's daughter – a ewe-lamb whiter, more precious than all of them – lay sleeping, trusting in my care. Never had the sky seemed to me so deep, never the stars so bright ... Suddenly, the gate of the fold opened and the lovely Stéphanette stood there beside me. She was not able to sleep. The sheep kept rustling the straw as they moved, or bleated in their dreams. She preferred to come by the fire. So I threw my goat-skin over her shoulders, I stirred up the fire, and we stayed seated side by side close to one another, without saying a word. If you have ever passed the night in the open under the stars, you will know that while we are sleeping a mysterious world awakens in the solitude and in the silence. Then the streams sing even more clearly, and on their pools dance little lights like flames. All the spirits of the mountains come and go as they will, and the air is filled with faint rustlings, imperceptible sounds, as if one were hearing the branches burgeoning and the grass growing. The day gives life to the world of humans and animals, but the night gives life to the world of things. And when one is not accustomed to this, it is frightening ... So my young mistress kept shuddering with fear and holding herself close to me at every slightest sound. Once, a long, melancholy cry rose and fell again and again from the pool gleaming below us. At the same time, a beautiful shooting star passed overhead across the pool, and it was as if that sad cry and that beautiful light were each bearing the other with it.

'What is that?' Stéphanette whispered to me.

'A soul entering Paradise, mistress.' And I made the sign of the cross.

She crossed herself also, and remained a moment with her head raised, lost in her thoughts. Then she said:

'So it is true that all you shepherds are sorcerers?'

'Most certainly it isn't, mistress. But up here we live nearer to the stars and we know what happens among them better than the people of the plains.'

She still kept looking up at the sky, her chin resting on her hand, wrapped in the goat-skin like a little shepherd from Paradise herself.

'What a lot there are! And how beautiful! I've never seen so many ... Do you know their names, shepherd?'

'Of course, mistress ... Look, right above us, is *Saint James's Way* (The Milky Way). From France it goes straight over to Spain. Saint James of Galicia set it there to show our wonderful Charlemagne the way when he was fighting the Saracens. Further on, you can see *The Chariot of Souls* (The Great Bear) with its four shining axles. The three stars at the front are *The Three Beasts*, and that very small one, close to the third, is *The Charioteer*. Do you see that shower of falling stars all around it? They are the souls the good Lord does not want with Him ... And there, a little lower down, is *The Rake* or *The Three Kings* (Orion). We shepherds use them as our clock. Just by looking up at them, I can tell that it's now past midnight. A little lower still, to the south, you can see *John of Milan* (Sirius) burning like a torch. The shepherds tell a story about that star. One night, they say, *John of Milan* with *The Three Kings* and *The Chicken Coop* (The Pleiades) were invited to the wedding of a star who was a friend of theirs. *The Chicken Coop*, the most eager, set off first and took the upper road. There it is, up there, right at the top of the sky. *The Three Kings* took a lower road and caught up with him; but that lazy fellow, *John of Milan*, who had slept late, was left behind and was so annoyed he threw his staff after them to stop them. That is why *The Three Kings* are also called *John of Milan's Staff* ... But the most beautiful of all the stars, mistress, is our own star, *The Shepherd's Star*, which lights us at dawn when we go out with our flocks, and in the evening also when we return with them. We sometimes call it *Maguelonne*, the beautiful Maguelonne, who runs after *Peter of Provence* (Saturn) and gets married to him, every seven years.'

'What! The stars get married, shepherd?'

'Oh, yes, mistress.'

And while I was trying to explain to her about these marriages, I felt something entirely beautiful resting lightly on my shoulder. With a sweet crumpling of her ribbons and laces and of the curls of her hair, she had laid her sleeping head on my arm. We stayed thus, without moving, until the stars paled, dimmed by the dawning day. And I looked and looked at her as she slept, vaguely disturbed deep down within me, yet miraculously protected by the night's clear holy light which has never given me any thoughts but beautiful ones. Around us, the stars continued their silent march, as orderly as a great flock of sheep; and, at times, it seemed to me that one of these stars, the loveliest and the brightest, having lost her way, had come to lie on my shoulder in order to sleep . . .

6

The Girl from Arles

ON the way down to the village from my windmill you pass a farmhouse, built near the road at the far end of a large courtyard planted with African lotus trees. It is a real Provençal farmer's house with its red tiles, its wide expanse of irregularly placed windows, its lofty wind-vane and its pulley for hoisting the bundles of hay, brown wisps of which cling everywhere . . .

Why did this house fill me with such a feeling of horror? Why did the sight of its large closed gateway make my heart contract? I could not have said why, yet this house caused shivers to run down my spine. It looked too silent . . . No dogs barked as you passed, even the guinea-fowl used to run to hide noiselessly. Never the sound of voices from inside. Nothing, not even the sound of a mule-bell . . . But for the white window curtains and the smoking chimneys, you would have thought the place uninhabited.

Yesterday, at the stroke of midday I was returning from the village, and, to avoid the sun, I was walking close to the wall of the farm in the shade of the trees . . . On the road in front of the farmhouse some workmen were silently loading a cart with hay. The large door had been left open. As I passed I glanced inside and I saw at the back of the court-yard – with his elbows on a broad stone table and his head in his hands – a big white-haired old man. He was wearing breeches that were in tatters and a jacket that was too small for him. I stopped.

'Ssh! It's the master,' one of the men whispered to me. 'He's been like that since the death of his son.'

77

Just then a woman and a little boy, dressed in black and carrying big, gilt prayer-books, passed close to us and entered the farm . . .

The man added:

'The mistress and the younger son coming back from Mass. They go every day since the boy killed himself . . . Ah, monsieur, what an affliction! . . . His father still wears the dead boy's clothes; nobody can stop him wearing them . . . Get along there!'

The cart began to move off. Wishing to know more, I asked the driver if I could get up beside him. And it was up there, on top of the hay, that I learnt the whole of this heart-breaking story . . .

His name was Jan. He was a fine country lad, twenty years old, open-faced, well-built, as gentle as a girl. Because of his good looks, the women used to follow him with their eyes, but he had eyes only for one of them – a girl from Arles, all in velvet and lace, whom he had met one day beside the Lice in Arles. At first everybody at the farm was not pleased. The girl was said to be flighty and her parents were not local people. But Jan was determined to have his girl from Arles. He used to say:

'I will die if she is not mine.'

The situation had to be accepted. It was agreed they should be married after the harvest.

Well, one Sunday evening, the family were just finishing dinner in the courtyard. It was almost a wedding feast. The fiancée was not there, but many glasses had been drunk in her honour . . . Then a man appears at the door and in a trembling voice asks to speak to the farmer Estève, by himself. Estève gets up and goes out on to the roadway.

'Master,' says the man, 'you are marrying your son to a hussy who has been my mistress for two years. What I say I can prove: see these letters! Her parents know and they had

78

promised her to me, but ever since your son has kept pester-
ing her, her fine ladyship and her parents don't want anything more to do with me ... But I'd have thought, after
what these letters show, she couldn't become the wife of
another man.'

Estève looks at the letters.

'That settles it,' he says. 'Come in and have a glass of
muscatel.'

The man replies:

'Thank you, but I am not thirsty, only full of sorrow.'

And he goes away.

The father goes back in, his face betraying nothing; he
takes his place again at the table; and the meal continues
merrily ...

That evening, Estève and his son went out together into
the fields. They stayed out a long time. When they came
back, the mother was still waiting for them.

'Wife,' said the farmer, leading his son to her, 'take him
to you! He is very unhappy ...'

Jan never mentioned the girl from Arles again. But he
loved her still; more even, since they had proved to him she
had lain in the arms of another. It was simply that he was
too proud to say anything; that is what killed him, poor
boy! ... Sometimes he would pass whole days sitting alone
in a corner. Other times he would go out on to the land and
do furiously, by himself, the work of ten labourers ... In
the evening, he would take the road to Arles and walk on
and on until he saw the slender steeples of the town rising
against the sunset. Then he would turn back. Never did he
go any further.

Seeing him like this, always sad and alone, the people at
the farm did not know what to do. They began to dread
some disaster ... Once, during dinner, his mother looked at
him, her eyes full of tears, and said:

'All right! Listen, Jan, if you still want her, you shall have her . . .'

His father flushed and looked down, overcome by the shame of it.

Jan shook his head and went out . . .

From that day his attitude changed. He pretended to be always cheerful, in order to reassure his parents. He was seen again at dances, in taverns, at bull-brandings. At the fair at Fontvieille* it was he who led the farandole.

The father kept saying:

'He's got over it.' The mother still had her forebodings and watched her boy more than ever . . . Jan slept with his younger brother, quite near the silkworm rearing-house; the poor old woman had a bed made for her next to their room . . . The silkworms might need her, in the night.

Then came the feast of St Eloi, patron of farmers.

Great rejoicings at the farm . . . There was châteauneuf for everybody, and mulled wine flowed like water. Fireworks followed, bonfires in the yard, and coloured lanterns hung on all the trees . . . Long live St Eloi! Everybody danced the farandole until they dropped. The younger son burnt his new smock. Jan himself actually looked happy; he danced with his mother; the poor woman wept for joy.

At midnight they went to bed. Everybody was ready to fall asleep on their feet . . . Everybody except Jan. His younger brother told later that all night Jan lay sobbing . . . Yes, he was still taking it very badly, poor lad.

Next day, at dawn, his mother heard somebody pass through her room, running. She knew at once something was wrong.

'Jan? Is that you?'

Jan does not reply; he is already on the stairs.

Quickly the mother gets up.

*See note on page 31.

'Jan! Where are you going?'

He goes up to the loft. She follows him.

'Jan, my boy, answer me. What are you doing?'

She gropes for the latch, her old hands trembling ... A window opening, a body falling on to the paving-stones of the yard and all is over.

The poor boy had said to himself:

'I love her too much ... I am going to go away from it all ...' Ah, what misery the human heart can bear. But there is one burden too heavy for it – to realize we cannot stop loving the woman we have come to despise.

That morning, the people of the village wondered who was crying out so, up at Estève's farm.

There, in the yard, in front of the dew-covered, blood-covered stone table, the mother, naked from her bed, was crying for her child, lying dead in her arms.

7

The Pope's Mule

OF all the striking sayings, proverbs and adages with which our peasants of Provence flavour their talk, I know none more picturesque and unusual than this one. For fifteen leagues around my mill, when they speak of a spiteful, vindictive person, they say: 'Beware of that man! He's like the Pope's mule who saved up her kick for seven years.'

For a long time I searched for the source of this proverb about a papal mule who kept a kick for somebody for seven years. Nobody here could enlighten me, not even Francet Mamai, my fife-player, who has all the legends of Provence at his finger tips. Francet thought, as I did, that it must be based on some ancient tale of the people of Avignon, but he had never heard anything except the proverb.

'You'll only find out about that one from the cicadas' library,' the old fife-player said, with a laugh.

The suggestion seemed a good one, and as the cicadas' library is at my door, I went and browsed in it for a week.

It is a marvellous library admirably arranged, open day and night to poets, and looked after by little librarians with cymbals who make music all the time for you. I spent several delightful days there, and after a week's research – on my back – I finally found what I was looking for, the story of my mule and this famous kick she kept for seven years. It's a charming little tale, if a little naïve, and I will try to tell it to you just as I read it yesterday morning in a manuscript, the colour of the time of the year, which smelt sweetly of dried lavender and had long gossamer threads for bookmarks.

*

Whoever did not see Avignon in the days of the Popes*
has seen nothing. There was never such a town for life,
bustle, gaiety and endless feast-days. From morning till
night there were processions, pilgrimages, streets strewn
with flowers and hung with high-warp tapestries, arrivals of
Cardinals, banners flying in the wind, flags flying from
galleys on the Rhône, the Pope's soldiers singing in Latin in
the squares, the rattles of the begging friars. And from all
the high houses crowded around the great Papal Palace,
there was heard a continual humming and buzzing: lace-
makers' needles clicking and weavers' shuttles darting,
making fold-threaded vestments; little hammers tapping,
shaping communion vessels for the altars; sounding boards
twanging, being turned by the lute-makers; women at their
looms all singing hymns. Louder still, there rose the noise
of the bells, and always the long, narrow drums of Provence
were to be heard kicking up a din down there on the bridge.
Because in our country, when people are happy they must
dance, and since at that time the streets of the town were
too narrow for the farandole, fife-players and drummers
took up positions on the bridge of Avignon in the fresh wind
sweeping down the Rhône, and day and night everybody
danced there, everybody danced there . . . Ah, what happy
times! And what a happy, happy town! Halberds that did
not cut, state-prisons where wine was put to keep cool. No
famines, no wars . . . That was how the Popes of Avignon
governed their people; that was why their people missed
them so greatly when they had gone! . . .

There was one of them in particular, a good old man
called Boniface . . .† Many tears indeed were shed for him

---

*Avignon was the residence of the Popes from 1309 to 1377 during
which time the city enjoyed great splendour and prosperity.

†A fictitious person. Of the seven Popes who resided at Avignon,
none was called Boniface.

in Avignon when he died! Such a friendly, such an affable prince, he was! He would joke with you so pleasantly from up on the back of his mule. And when you passed near him – even though you were a poor little madder-gatherer, or the chief provost of the town – he would give you his blessing so civilly! A true prince of the church, but a prince of Provence, whose laugh hid a certain shrewdness, whose biretta had a sprig of sweet marjoram in it, and for whom serving wenches had no attraction. The only thing to which this good father was known to be devoted was his vineyard – a little vineyard he had planted himself, three leagues from Avignon, among the myrtles of Château Neuf.

Every Sunday, when he came out from Vespers, the good man would go and visit the object of his affection, and when he was up there, seated in the warm sunshine, with his mule near him, and his cardinals reclining around him at the foot of the vines, then he would have a bottle of his own wine opened – that beautiful wine, the colour of rubies, which has ever since been known as Château-Neuf des Papes – and he would savour it slowly in little sips, whilst gazing around fondly at his vineyard. Then, the bottle empty and evening drawing on, he would return happily to the town, followed by all his chapter. And when he passed over the bridge of Avignon, amid the drums and the farandoles, his mule, aroused by the music, would begin to amble skippingly, while the Pope himself would beat time to the dance with his biretta, thus greatly scandalizing his cardinals, but causing all the people to say: 'Oh, what a kind prince! What a good Pope!'

After his vineyard at Château-Neuf, what the Pope loved most in the world was his mule. The good man made a complete fool of the beast. Every evening before going to bed, he used to go to her stall to make sure her door was shut and her manger full of food. And he'd never leave the table without seeing with his own eyes a great bowl of wine prepared, with plenty of sugar and spice in the French fashion. This he would then carry to his mule himself, despite all the comments of his cardinals . . . It must be admitted nevertheless that the animal was worth it. She was a beautiful mule, black with red flecks, sure-footed, with a glossy coat and a full broad back. She carried proudly her shapely little head, adorned with tassels, knots, bows and silver bells. Added to that, she was as gentle as an angel, with guileless eyes and long ears, always flapping, that gave her a good-natured look. All Avignon respected her and when she went along the streets every kind of courteous attention was paid her, for everyone knew that that was the best way of finding favour at court, that with her innocent look the Pope's mule had led more than one person to fortune, as was proved by Tistet Védène and his stupendous adventure.

From the very beginning, this Tistet Védène was an impudent young ne'er-do-well, whom his father, the sculptor in gold, Guy Védène, had had to turn out of his house because he wouldn't work and kept leading the apprentices into trouble. For six months he was seen loafing about the streets of Avignon, chiefly in the neighbourhood of the Papal Palace, since for quite a while the young rascal had had his own ideas about the papal mule, and quite cunning ideas they were too, as you shall see . . .

One day when His Holiness was riding on his mule along the ramparts all by himself, who should happen to meet him but our Tistet. And what should our Tistet do but clasp his hands together in admiration and exclaim:

'Good Heavens! What a fine mule you've got, Holy Father! . . . Do let me look at her a little . . . Oh, Your Holiness, what a mule, what a mule! . . . Even the Emperor of Germany hasn't her equal.'

And he stroked her gently and spoke soft words to her as to a young girl.

'Come, my jewel, my treasure, my precious pearl . . .'
And the good Pope, deeply moved, said to himself:
'What a nice boy! . . . To be so kind to my mule! . . .'
And then do you know what happened next day? Tistet
Védène exchanged his old yellow coat for a beautiful lace
alb, a surplice cape in violet silk, and buckled shoes, and he
entered the Pope's choir school, where before him only the
sons of noblemen and the nephews of cardinals had been

admitted as pupils. So you see what cunning can achieve!
. . . But Tistet did not stop there.

Once he was in the Pope's service, the scalliwag continued to play the game which had proved so successful.
Insolent to everybody, he paid no attention to anyone but
the mule and he was always to be found in the palace courtyards with a handful of oats or a bundle of sainfoin whose
pink clusters he would shake gently as he looked up at the
Holy Father's balcony, as much as to say: 'Now, who do
you think this is for?' . . . So in the end it came about that
the Pope, who felt himself growing old, entrusted to Tistet
the care of the stables, and allowed him to carry the mule's
bowl of spiced wine to her, which did not make the
cardinals laugh at all.

Nor, as you shall see, was it a laughing matter for the
mule . . . When the time for her wine arrived, there would
now always first appear five or six little choir boys who
would squat down quickly on the hay in their capes and their
surplices. A moment later, a nice warm smell of caramel and
spice would spread through the stable and Tistet would
appear, carefully carrying the bowl of wine. The martyrdom
of the poor animal would then begin.

The scented wine which she loved so much, which kept
her warm, which gave her wings, they were so cruel as to
bring right up to her and allow her to sniff. Then, when she
was overcome with the smell of it, every drop of that
beautiful rose-red liquid would disappear down those little
rascals' throats . . . And then, as if stealing her wine were
not enough, after they had drunk it those little choir boys
became little devils. One of them would pull her ears,
another would pull her tail. Quiquet would get up on her
back, Béluguet would stick his biretta on her, and not one
of those young scamps ever stopped to think that, with a
single twist of her hindquarters and one flying kick, the
good creature could have sent them all to the Pole-Star and

even further . . . But no! Not for nothing was she the Pope's mule, the mule of blessings and indulgences . . . Whatever those boys did, she did not lose control of herself; though she would have liked to with one of them . . . Whenever she sensed Tistet Védène was behind her, she felt an itching in her hoof, and there was every reason that she should. That good-for-nothing Tistet played such vicious tricks on her! The wine gave him such cruel ideas . . .

One day, what should come into his head but to pull her after him up the bell-turret of the choir school, high up to the very topmost point of the palace! . . . And this is not a tale I'm making up for you, two hundred thousand people of Provence saw it. Imagine to yourself the terror of that unhappy mule, when, having turned blindly round and round for an hour up a spiral staircase, and climbed I don't know how many steps, she found herself suddenly on a platform in a blaze of light and saw spread out a thousand feet below her a completely fantastic Avignon, the market stalls no bigger than nuts, the Pope's soldiers in front of their barracks like ants, and away down there on a silver thread a microscopically little bridge where people danced . . . Oh, the poor, panic-stricken animal! The cry of terror she let forth made every window of the palace shake.

'What's the matter? What are they doing to her?' shouted the good Pope, rushing out on to his balcony.

Tistet Védène was already in the courtyard, pretending to weep and tear his hair.

'Oh, Holy Father! What a thing to happen! It's your mule . . . Oh, heavens, how can such things happen? Your mule has climbed the bell-turret! . . .'

'What! All by herself???'

'Yes, Holy Father, all by herself. Up there, look! Do you see the tips of her ears? You'd think they were two swallows . . .'

'Oh, mercy upon us!' exclaimed the Pope, looking up.

'But she must have gone mad! She'll kill herself . . . Come down at once, you foolish animal! . . .'

Alas! There was nothing she wanted to do more . . . but how? The staircase was out of the question: those things can be climbed, but getting down them could break one's legs a hundred times . . . The poor mule was in despair and as she went to and fro on the platform, her big eyes glazed with vertigo, she kept thinking of Tistet Védène:

'Oh, the villain! If I get out of this alive, what a kick he's going to get tomorrow morning!'

The thought of this kick restored her courage a little; without the thought of it she would not have been able to hold out . . . At last, they succeeded in bringing her down; but it was quite a business. It was necessary to lower her by means of a pulley, ropes and a sling. You can imagine what a humiliation it was for a Pope's mule to be dangling in the air at that height, waving her legs in space like a beetle on the end of a string. And with all Avignon watching her!

The poor animal did not sleep that night. It seemed to her she was still wandering round on that accursed platform, with all the town shaking with laughter below her. Then she would think of that scoundrel Tistet Védène and of the beautiful kick she would let loose at him the next morning. Oh, what a kick that was going to be, my friends! They would see the smoke from it as far away as Pampérigouste . . . But, whilst this stupendous kick was being prepared for him in the stable, do you know what Tistet Védène was doing? He was singing on board a papal galley as it sailed down the Rhône to the Court of Naples with the company of young nobles the town sent each year to Queen Jeanne to be trained in diplomacy and courtly manners. Tistet was not of noble birth, but the Pope had insisted on rewarding him for the care he had taken of his mule, and most especially for the zeal he had just shown during the work of rescue.

It was the mule who was greatly put out next morning!

'The villain! He suspected something!' she thought, shaking her bells furiously. 'All right, you rogue! You'll find your kick still here when you get back . . . I'll keep it for you!'

And she kept it for him.

After Tistet's departure, the Pope's mule went back to her quiet life, to all the pleasures she had formerly enjoyed. No more of Quiquet and Béluguet in the stable! The good old days of spiced wine came back again, and with them her good humour, her long siestas, and her little gavotte as she ambled across the bridge of Avignon. Nevertheless, ever since her adventure, a slight coldness on the part of the townspeople was noticeable. As she passed by, people whispered, old women shook their heads, and children used to laugh and point to the bell-turret. The good Pope himself no longer had the same confidence in his friend, and, whenever he allowed himself a short nap as he rode home on her from the vineyard on Sundays, there was always the thought at the back of his mind: 'Suppose I woke up and found myself up there on top of the bell-turret!' The mule saw all this and suffered it all silently; only, whenever the name of Tistet Védène was mentioned in front of her, her long ears used to quiver and with a little laugh she would sharpen the iron of her hoofs on the paving-stones.

Thus did seven years pass. Then, at the end of these seven years, Tistet Védène came back from the Court of Naples. His time there was still not finished, but he had heard that the First Bearer of the Pope's Mustard Pot* had died suddenly at Avignon, and, as it seemed just the right post for him, he arrived back in great haste in order to get in first.

When this schemer entered the great hall of the Palace,

*Apparently Pope John XXII created such a post for his nephew, and it does not of course exist today. The name has come to mean a person who thinks a great deal of himself.

the Pope had difficulty in recognizing him, so much taller and stouter had he grown. It must also be said, on his side, the Pope had grown old and did not see well without his spectacles.

Tistet did not allow himself to become nervous:

'What, Holy Father! You don't recognize me? It's me, Tistet Védène!...'

'Védène?'

'Yes, you know ... I used to take your mule her spiced wine.'

'Ah!... yes ... yes ... I remember ... Tistet Védène ... yes, he was a nice little lad ... Yes, now, what is it he wants from us?'

'Oh, just a small thing, Holy Father ... I was wondering ... By the way, have you still got your mule? And is she keeping well? Oh, good! I'm so glad!... Yes, well, I was wondering if you would let me have the post of the First Mustard Cup Bearer who has just died.'

'First Mustard Cup Bearer! You!... But you are too young! How old are you?'

'Twenty years and two months, Illustrious Pontiff. Exactly five years older than your mule ... Oh, that wonderful animal, how I missed her in Italy!... Won't you allow me to see her?'

'Yes, my son, you shall see her,' the good Pope exclaimed, deeply moved. 'And since you are so fond of the dear creature, I don't wish you to be living so far away from her. From this day forth, I attach you to my person as First Bearer of the Mustard Pot. My cardinals will start shouting, but I don't care! I'm used to that. Come and see me tomorrow after Vespers and I shall bestow upon you the insignia of your office in the presence of the whole Chapter, and then ... I shall take you to see my mule and you shall accompany us both to the vineyard ... Yes, yes! It will be as you wish! Leave us now ...'

So Tistet Védène went out of the great hall a happy man and I've no need to tell you how impatiently he now awaited the morrow's ceremony. Yet there was someone in the palace even happier and even more impatient than he: and that was the mule. From the moment Védène came back, until Vespers the following day, the terrible beast did not stop stuffing herself with oats and letting fly with her hoofs at the wall behind her. She, too, was getting ready for the ceremony.

So the next day, after Vespers, Tistet Védène made his entrance into the Courtyard of the Papal Palace. All the higher clergy were there, the cardinals in their scarlet robes, the devil's advocate in his black velvet, the abbots of the monastery with their little mitres, the churchwardens from the church of St Agricol, the violet capes of the choir boys, the lower clergy too, the Pope's soldiers in full uniform, the three Brotherhoods of the penitents, the wild-looking hermits from Mont Ventoux and the little clerk who brings up the rear carrying the little bell, the Flagellant Brothers naked to the waist, the florid sacristans in their judges' robes, they were all there, all of them, even the givers of holy water, the lighters of candles, and those who extinguish candles . . . not one of them was missing . . . It was indeed a most wonderful ordination! Bells were ringing, fireworks cracking, the sun was shining and music playing, and always the wild beating of those drums that were leading the dance, down below, on the bridge of Avignon . . .

When Védène appeared in the midst of this assembly, his noble bearing and handsome looks aroused a murmur of admiration. He was a magnificent son of Provence, of the blond type, with long hair which curled at the ends, and a little, curly beard that seemed to consist of the shavings of precious metal fallen from the graving-tool of his father, the sculptor in gold. Rumour had it that the fingers of Queen Jeanne had sometimes played with that beard, and my lord

Védène had indeed the proud look and careless glance of those men whom queens have loved ... On this day, in honour of his native land of Provence, he had replaced his Neapolitan clothes with a coat bordered with pink in the Provençal style, and, on his sleeved cap, there quivered a long ibis feather from the Camargue.

As soon as he had entered, the First Bearer of the Mustard Pot bowed elegantly, and advanced towards the lofty flight of steps on which the Pope was waiting to invest him with the insignia of his office: the spoon of yellow box-wood and the saffron coat. The mule was at the foot of the steps, harnessed and ready to depart for the vineyard ... As he passed near her, Tistet Védène had a smile on his face and stopped to give her two or three friendly little pats on her back, looking out of the corner of his eye to see if the Pope was watching. The position was just right ... The mule let loose:

'There! Take that, villain! Seven years I've kept that for you!'

And the kick she let fly was so terrible, so terrible, that in far-off Pampérigouste* they saw the smoke of it, vast clouds of yellow smoke in which there fluttered an ibis feather; all that was left of the unfortunate Tistet Védène!

Mule's kicks are not usually so annihilating; but this was a papal mule; besides, you must not forget she had been saving it for him for seven years ... There cannot be a more perfect example of clerical rancour.

*See note on page 42.

8

The Lighthouse of *Les Sanguinaires*

LAST night I could not sleep. The mistral was in a bad temper, and the roaring of its loud voice kept me awake till morning. The whole mill kept creaking and the tattered sails, swinging heavily, whistled in the wind like the rigging of a ship. Tiles flew off its crumbling roof. In the distance, the close-packed pines that clothe the hill tossed and swished noisily in the darkness. You could have believed yourself out on the open sea . . .

It brought back to me so clearly those splendid vigils I used to keep three years ago, when I was living in the light-house of *Les Sanguinaires*, over there on the coast of Corsica, at the entrance to the Gulf of Ajaccio.

There I had found another pleasant corner in which to dream and to be alone.

Picture to yourself a grim little island of reddish-coloured rocks, with the lighthouse at one end and at the other an ancient Genoese tower in which, when I was there, there lodged an eagle. In between, down by the edge of the sea there stood the ruins of an old naval quarantine station, all overgrown with grass and weeds; around it, ravines, maquis, rocks, wild goats, small Corsican horses galloping with their manes flying in the wind; and then, high, high up there, in a swirling, tossing mass of sea-birds, the lighthouse, with its platform of white stone where the keepers walk to and fro, its green, arched doorway, its cast-iron tower, and, on top, the huge, many-sided lantern that glitters flame-like in the sun and gives out light, even during the day . . . Such was the island of *Les Sanguinaires*, as I saw it again last night listening to the roaring of my pines. It was to this island I used to go, before I had my windmill, when I felt the need of fresh air and solitude.

What did I use to do there?

What I do here, more or less. When the mistral or the tramontane did not blow too strongly, I used to settle down between two rocks near the water's edge, among the sea-gulls, the water-ousels, and the swallows, and there I would remain for almost the whole day in that soporific stupor, that languid sense of delight which comes from just looking at the sea. You must have experienced it, surely, that wonderful rapture of the spirit? You cease to think, even to dream. Your innermost self escapes, flying, drifting. You become the seagull swooping, the frothing foam floating in the sun between two waves, the white smoke of the liner far-off on the horizon, that little red-sailed, coral-fishing boat, this pearly drop of water, this drifting wisp of mist, you become everything but yourself . . . Oh, those wonderful hours I spent on my island, drifting, drifting, half-asleep! . . .

On days of high wind, when the water's edge was out of the question, I would shut myself away in the courtyard of the old quarantine station, a gloomy little courtyard, full of the smell of rosemary and wild absinthe, and huddled there against a bit of old wall, I would let myself be gently over-whelmed by the vaguely scented emanations of desuetude and sadness that hovered in the sunshine over the little stone cells which gaped all around me like ancient bombs. Now and then a door banged, the grass quivered . . . and a goat would come to feed out of the wind. On seeing me, she would stop quite disconcerted and stay, rooted to the ground, all alert, horns raised, looking at me with child-like eyes . . .

About five o'clock, the lighthouse keepers' megaphone would summon me to dinner. I would then take a little path through the maquis that rose steeply from the sea and I would return slowly to the lighthouse, turning at each step to gaze at that immense horizon of water and of light that seemed to grow wider and wider as I climbed.

Up there in the lighthouse it was delightful. I can see still its fine dining-room with its wide flag-stones, its oak panelling, the bouillabaisse steaming on the table, the door flung wide open on to the white terrace and all the glory of the setting sun . . . The lighthouse keepers would be there, waiting for me before taking their seats at the table. There were three of them: one from Marseilles and two from Corsica, all small, bearded, their faces lined and weather-beaten, wearing similar short jackets of goat-skin, but completely different in manner and temperament.

The difference between them could be seen at once from their mode of life. The man from Marseilles, active, hard-working, always busy, always on the move, hastening about the island from morn till night, gardening, fishing, gathering sea-birds' eggs, lying in wait in the maquis to catch a goat and milk her; and always with some mayonnaise with garlic or some bouillabaisse in the making.

But the Corsicans, beyond their official duties they did absolutely nothing; they considered themselves to be civil servants and spent their days in the kitchen playing interminable games of cards, stopping only to light their pipes with a serious air, or to cut big leaves of green tobacco with a pair of scissors into the palms of their hands . . .

Apart from all this, all three were kindly fellows, simple, guileless, and full of attentions for their guest, though he must have seemed to them a most extraordinary person . . .

To come and shut himself up in a lighthouse just for the pleasure of it! What must they have thought of him, they who found the days so long and who were so happy when their turn came to go back to the mainland? In the fine season of the year this great good fortune is theirs once a month. Ten days ashore to every thirty days on the lighthouse, that is the rule; but in winter and during bad weather, all rules go by the board. The wind blows and the sea rises, *Les Sanguinaires* is white with foam, and the keepers on duty are stuck there for two or three months on end, and sometimes under the most terrible conditions.

'This is what happened to me personally, monsieur,' old Bartoli related to me one day, while we were having dinner. 'This is what happened to me five years ago, at this very table where we are now, one winter's evening, just like this one. That evening there were only two of us in the lighthouse, myself and a comrade everyone called "Tchéco" . . . The others were ashore, sick, off duty, I don't remember . . . We were finishing dinner, just like every night . . . Suddenly, my comrade stops eating, looks at me a moment, his eyes all strange, and then down he drops on to the table with his arms all spread out. So I go over to him. I shake him. I call him:

'"Tché! . . . Tché! . . ."

'No answer! He was dead! . . . You can guess how I felt! I sat there, beside his body for an hour, stunned and trembling. Then suddenly the thought came to me: "The light!" I just had time to climb up to the lantern and light it as night fell. And what a night, monsieur! I know the voices of the wind and the sea, but that night they didn't sound natural. I kept thinking I could hear someone calling to me from down the stairs. I became feverish. And thirsty! But nothing would have made me go down those stairs again . . . I was too frightened of that dead man. However, when dawn came, my courage returned a little. I went down and carried my comrade to his bed, put a sheet over him, said a little prayer, and then quickly sent out the alarm signal.

'Unfortunately, the seas were too high: I sent it out again

and again; nobody came ... There I was alone in the light-house with my poor Tchéco, heaven knew for how long ... At first I kept hoping I would be able to keep him there until the boat came! But after three days that became impossible ... What was I to do? Carry him outside? Bury him? The rock was so hard, and there were so many crows on the island. He was a Christian and I couldn't think of abandoning his body to the crows ... Then I thought of putting him in one of the cells in the quarantine station. It took me a whole afternoon, that sad task, and I can tell you it needed some courage. Yes, monsieur, even today when I go down to that side of the island, on an afternoon when the wind's high, I feel as if I still had that dead man on my shoulders...'

Poor old Bartoli! Just from thinking of it, the sweat was running down his forehead.

We used to talk for a long time over our meals about such things: about the lighthouse, the sea, tales of shipwreck, stories of Corsican bandits ... Then, dusk falling, the keeper who had to take the first watch would light his little lamp, pick up his pipe, his water-bottle, the thick red-bound volume of Plutarch, the only book on *Les Sanguinaires*, and disappear up the stairs. A few moments later, the whole lighthouse started echoing with the rattling of chains and pulleys as the pendulum weights of the lantern were set in motion.

While this was being done, I would go out and sit on the terrace. The sun, already well down, would descend quicker and quicker into the sea, drawing the whole horizon after it. The wind used to freshen, the island become the colour of violet. Near me, in the sky, a huge bird would pass slowly, heavily: the eagle of the Genoese tower returning to its home ... Little by little the mist would rise over the sea. Soon nothing was visible save the white fringe of foam surrounding the island ... Suddenly, above my head, there would pour out a great flood of soft light. The lantern was lit. Leaving all the island in darkness, that clear beam stretched far and wide out to sea, and there, below its piercing bright rays, which barely touched me, I would sit on, lost in the night ... But at last the wind would grow stronger and colder and I'd have to go in again. Feeling with my hands, I would shut the great door and replace the iron bars. Then still feeling my way, I would climb a narrow iron staircase which shook and rang under my feet. At last the darkness gave way to light, and what a light it was.

Imagine a gigantic Carcel lamp with six rows of wicks, around which revolve slowly the lantern's walls, some fitted with enormous lenses, others with great fixed mirrors which shelter the flames from the wind ... At first I would be dazzled. The shining tinfoil, the copper brasses, the white metal reflectors, the convex crystal walls turning in great bluish circles, all the flashing, clashing lights, would make me feel dizzy for a few moments.

Gradually, however, my eyes would get used to it, and I would go and sit right at the foot of the lamp beside the keeper, who would be reading his Plutarch aloud, for fear he fell asleep ...

Outside, the night, the dark abyss. On the little balcony which encircles the glass casing of the lantern the wind screams and howls like a madman. The lighthouse creaks, the sea roars. At the tip of the island, on the half-submerged rocks, the waves make a noise like cannon fire ... At intervals, an invisible finger taps on the panes: some night bird, attracted by the light, has dashed itself against the crystal glass ... Inside the lantern of the lighthouse, all is warm and bright: only the sounds of the crackling flames, the oil dripping, the chain unwinding, and the monotonous voice intoning the life of Demetrius of Phalerum.

*

At midnight, the keeper used to rise, throw a last glance at the wicks, and he would descend. On the stairs we would meet the keeper on the second watch, rubbing his eyes as he came up; he would be given the water-bottle, the Plutarch ... Then, before finding our beds, we used to go into the back room, and there, amidst the clutter of chains, weights, tin reflectors, ropes, and by the light of his little lamp, the keeper would write in the big lighthouse log book, which is kept always open:

'Midnight. High seas. Gale. Ship sighted well away from coast.'

9

The Agony of *La Sémillante*

SINCE the mistral the other night has cast us up on the Corsican coast, allow me to tell you a dreadful tale of the sea, which fishermen down there talk about in guarded voices when evening comes, and about which chance furnished me with some very strange pieces of information.

. . . That happened two or three years ago.

I was sailing around the Sardinian Sea in company with seven or eight sailors of the customs service. A rough voyage for a novice. During the whole of March we did not have one good day. An east wind hounded us relentlessly and the sea never stopped raging furiously.

One evening as we were fleeing before the storm, we took shelter in the entrance to the straits of Bonifacio amid a lot of little islands. There was certainly nothing attractive about them: great, bare rocks, covered with birds, a few tufts of absinthe, lentisk bushes, and here and there in the mud pieces of rotting wood. But I give you my word, those evil-looking rocks were a better place to spend that night in than the deck-house of an old, half-decked boat which allowed the sea to enter like a welcomed guest. We were quite content to be there.

We had hardly got ashore, and the sailors were busy lighting a fire, when the captain called to me and pointed to a little enclosure surrounded by white stone walls, almost hidden in the mist at the other end of the little island:

'Are you coming over to the cemetery?' he said to me.

'Cemetery, Captain Lionetti! Where are we then?'

'In the Lavezzi Islands, monsieur. The six hundred men from *La Sémillante* are buried here, where their frigate went down ten years ago . . . Poor fellows! They don't get many visitors; now that we're here, it's the least we can do to go and say good-day to them . . .'

'With all my heart, captain.'

How sad it was, the cemetery of *La Sémillante*! . . . I see it still with its little low wall, its rusty iron gate, hard to open, its silent chapel, and the hundreds of black crosses, hidden in the grass. Not one wreath, not a sign of remembrance anywhere! Nothing . . . How cold they must lie, in their fortuitous graves, those poor abandoned dead!

We stayed there a moment, on our knees. The captain prayed aloud. Enormous gulls, sole guardians of the cemetery, swooped circling above our heads, mingling their hoarse cries with the lamentations of the sea.

The prayer finished, we went back to the corner of the island where the ship was moored. In our absence, the sailors had not been wasting their time. We found a big fire blazing in the shelter of a rock and the pot steaming. We all sat around it, our feet to the flames, and soon each of us had on our knees a red earthenware bowl containing two slices of black bread laced with sauce. The meal passed in silence: we were wet, hungry, and the cemetery was so near . . . However, when the bowls were empty, pipes were lit and gradually everyone began to talk. Naturally, it was of *La Sémillante* we spoke.

'But how did it happen?' I asked the captain, who was gazing thoughtfully into the flames, his hands cupped under his chin.

'How did it happen?' replied Lionetti, with a deep sigh. 'Alas, monsieur, not a living soul can tell you that. All that we know is that *La Sémillante*, laden with troops for the

Crimea, had left Toulon the evening before in bad weather. During the night the weather became worse. Wind, rain, enormous seas such as had never been seen before . . . In the morning the wind fell a little, but the seas were still as bad as ever, and on top of that there was a hellish fog so cursed thick that you couldn't see a lantern four paces away. No one, monsieur, can have any idea how treacherous those fogs can be . . . But my opinion is *La Sémillante* must have lost her rudder that morning, because the captain would never have landed her on these rocks, no matter how bad the fog was, unless her rudder had gone. We all knew him; he was a fine sailor. He'd had three years in charge of the Corsica station, and he knew this coast as well as I do, and I know it like the back of my hand since it's all I do know.'

'What time of day do they think *La Sémillante* perished?'

'It must have been about noon. Yes, monsieur, right in the middle of the day, but a midday as black as the mouth of hell . . . A customs man from this coast told me that about half-past eleven that morning he went outside to fasten one of the shutters of his cottage. His cap was carried away by the wind and, at the risk of being swept away himself by the seas, he began to crawl along the beach on his hands and knees after it. Customs men, you know, aren't rich and a cap costs money. He told me he happened to look up and saw quite close in the fog a big ship with all her canvas gone, driving before the wind in the direction of the Lavezzi Islands. The ship was moving so quickly the customs man hadn't time to see her properly. However, everything points to her being *La Sémillante*, since half an hour afterwards the shepherds of these islands heard on these very rocks . . . But there's the shepherd I'm speaking of, monsieur; he'll tell you about it himself . . . Good day, Palombo! . . . Come and warm yourself a little; don't be frightened.'

A man wearing a hood, whom I had seen prowling around

the fire and whom I'd thought was one of the crew, for I hadn't known there was a shepherd on the island, approached us fearfully.

He was an old, leprous-looking man, three-parts idiot, suffering from I don't know what scorbutic disease which gave him huge thick lips, horrible to see. It was explained to him with some difficulty what we wanted. Then, lifting up his diseased lip with his finger, the old man told us that on the day in question, towards noon, he had heard from his hut a dreadful cracking sound on the rocks. As all the island was under water, he had not been able to go out and it was only the following morning on opening his door that he had seen the shore covered with the wreckage and the dead bodies left by the sea. Terror-stricken, he had fled, had run to his boat and gone to Bonifacio to find someone.

Exhausted by the effort of talking so much, the shepherd seated himself by the fire, and the captain continued:

'Yes, monsieur, it was this poor old man who came to tell us. He was nearly mad with the fright of it and has never been the same man since. In fact, it was enough to drive anyone out of their mind. Imagine six hundred corpses piled on the sand all mixed up with pieces of the sails and bits of wood ... Poor *Sémillante*! ... the sea had broken her at one blow, smashed her into so many little pieces that the shepherd Palombo was hardly able to find enough to make a fence around his hut ... As for the men, nearly all were disfigured, horribly mutilated ... it was pitiful to see them, lying in groups, clutching each other ... We found the captain in full uniform, the chaplain in his stole; and in one corner between two rocks there lay a little cabin boy with his eyes open ... we thought he was still alive; but no, it had been ordained that not one should escape! ...'

Here the captain interrupted himself:

'Watch out, there, Nardi!' he called. 'The fire's going down!'

Nardi threw two or three pieces of tarred planks on to the embers. They blazed up, and Lionetti went on:

'The saddest thing about it all was that three weeks before the disaster, a little corvette, bound for the Crimea like *La Sémillante*, had been wrecked in the same way and at almost the same spot. But, on that occasion, we had succeeded in rescuing the crew and twenty soldiers of the service corps who had been on board ... We took the soldiers back to Bonifacio and looked after them ourselves at the naval station for a couple of days. As soon as they'd dried out and got over the shock we wished them good luck and sent them off back to Toulon. Soon after, they were put on another ship to the Crimea ... Guess which ship it was ... *La Sémillante*, monsieur ... Yes, we found them all, all twenty of them, lying among the dead bodies. I myself picked up a corporal from Paris whom I'd put up at my house – a fine-looking fellow with a handsome moustache who'd kept us all laughing with his stories . . . To see him lying there, it broke my heart . . . Oh, Holy Mother of God! . . .'

And the good Lionetti, quite overcome, shook out the ashes from his pipe, wrapped himself up in his great coat and wished me good night. For a time the sailors went on talking among themselves in low voices . . . Then, one after another, the pipes went out . . . All talk ceased . . . The old shepherd went his way . . . And I was left alone among the sleeping crew with my thoughts . . .

Still greatly moved by the sad tale I had just heard, I tried to visualize in my mind that poor, shattered ship and the events of those agonizing hours of which the seagulls had been the only witnesses. The few details that had struck me, the captain in full uniform, the chaplain's stole, the twenty soldiers of the service corps, helped me to guess all the sequence of events of the tragedy . . . I saw the frigate leaving Toulon in the night . . . She sails out of the harbour . . . The sea is bad, the wind terrible, but the captain is an experienced sailor and everybody on board is calm . . .

In the morning, the sea-fog descends. Uneasiness spreads. All hands are aloft. The captain does not leave the poop-deck . . . 'Tween-decks, where the soldiers are shut in, all is dark and hot. Some are sick, lying on their packs. The ship pitches horribly and it is impossible to stand. The men talk sitting in groups, holding on to the benches. They have to shout to be heard. Some begin to be afraid . . . You wait and see, then! Shipwrecks are frequent in these waters! The service corps men have plenty to tell and what they tell is not reassuring. Their corporal especially, a Parisian who is always telling funny stories, makes their skin creep with his attempts at humour.

'Shipwreck! . . . It's great fun being shipwrecked! All you get is an ice-cold bath and then they take you to Bonifacio and you're given water-ousels to eat at Captain Lionetti's house!'

And the service corps men laugh.

There's suddenly a cracking sound . . . What is it? What is happening? . . .

'The rudder's beén carried away,' says a sailor, soaking wet, as he runs through 'tween-decks.

'Bon voyage!' shouts the mad corporal. But nobody laughs any more.

There is uproar up on the deck. It is hard to see anyone because of the fog. The terrified sailors grope their way with their hands . . . No rudder! Steering is impossible . . . *La Sémillante*, at the mercy of the waves, is driven headlong before the wind. It is at this moment that the customs man sees her pass; it is half-past eleven. Ahead of the frigate, a sound like cannon fire is heard. Breakers! Breakers on the rocks! . . . It is the end, all hope is gone, the ship is heading straight for the coast . . . The captain goes down to his cabin . . . and quickly reappears on the poop-deck – in full uniform . . . It is how he wishes to die.

'Tween-decks, the soldiers look at each other uneasily, saying nothing . . . The sick try to get up . . . the little corporal is no longer laughing . . . Then the door opens and the chaplain stands there, wearing his stole:

'On your knees, my children!'

All obey. His voice loud and strong, the priest begins the prayer for the dying.

Suddenly, a fearsome crunching crack, one cry, one single cry, one immense cry, outstretched arms, clutching hands, and in all those frightened eyes the vision of death passes like a flash of lightning . . .

'Lord have mercy upon us! . . .'

Thus did I pass all that night, seeing in my imagination that other night ten years before and summoning back the soul of the poor lost ship whose wrecked remains lay all around me ... In the straits, away in the distance, the storm was still raging; the flames of the camp-fire kept flickering low before the gale; and down below at the foot of the rocks, I could hear our boat tossing and straining loudly at her moorings.

10

The Customs Men

THE *Émilie*, of Porto-Vecchio, on board which I made this
melancholy voyage to the Lavezzi Islands, was a little old
customs boat, half-decked, with no protection from wind,
waves or rain, except for a little tarred deck-house hardly
wide enough to hold a table and two bunks. So, when the
weather was bad, our sailors were a sorry sight. Their faces
used to stream with water, their soaked jerseys to steam like
washing in a drying room, and in the midst of winter these
unfortunate men used to pass whole days in this condition,
whole nights even, crouched on their soaking benches,
shivering in this unhealthy dankness; for a fire could not be
lit on board and the shore was often difficult to reach . . .
Yet, not one of these men used to complain. During the
roughest weather, I saw them always serenely calm, im-
perturbedly good-humoured. All the same, no one lives
such a sad life as these customs men!

Almost all of them married, with wives and children
ashore, they remain at sea for months, beating to windward
along these very dangerous coasts. For food they have
scarcely anything beyond mouldy bread and wild onions.
Never any wine, never any meat, because meat and wine
cost much and they earn only five hundred francs a year!
You can imagine how gloomy the hut must be back there on
the sea shore and how the children must go bare-foot! . . .
And yet all these people seem content! There was at the
stern, in front of the deck-house, a large tub full of rain
water where the crew used to come to have a drink, and I
remember how, after the last mouthful, each of these poor

devils used to shake out his mug with an 'Ah!' of satisfaction, an expression of well-being at the same time both comical and pitiful.

The gayest, the most contented of them all was a little, thick-set, weather-beaten man from Bonifacio whom everybody called Palombo. This man was for ever singing, even during the very worst of weather. When the waves became large, when the dark lowering sky was full of frozen snow, and everybody was tensed, their hands on the sail, ready for the next squall, into the great silence and the anxiety of all on board, the untroubled voice of Palombo used to commence:

> No, no, no, good sir,
> 'Tis too great an honour,
> Sweet Lisette is goo – d
> Stays here as she shou – ld

And the squall could do its worst, could make the rigging creak and moan, could toss and flood the little boat, the song of the customs man went lilting on, rising and falling like a seagull on the crests of the waves. Sometimes the accompanying wind was too strong and we no longer heard the words, but, between each roaring sea, above the rushing sound of the water flowing away off the deck, the little refrain always came back again:

> Sweet Lisette is goo – d
> Stays here as she shou – ld

One day, however, when it was blowing and raining very heavily, I did not hear him. It was so unusual I put my head out of the deck-house:

'Eh! Palombo! No more songs?'

Palombo did not reply. He was motionless, stretched out on his bench. I went up to him. His teeth were chattering: his whole body was shaking with fever.

'He has a *pountoura*,' his friends sadly told me. What they call a *pountoura* is an acute pain in the side, pleurisy. This vast leaden sky, this boat streaming with water, this poor feverish man wrapped in an old rubber cloak which gleamed in the rain like the skin of a seal – I have never seen anything more melancholy. The cold, the wind, the buffeting of the waves rapidly aggravated his pain; we had to make for land.

Towards evening, after much time and effort, we entered a little harbour, barren and silent, the only sign of life a few seagulls circling overhead. All around rose high steep rocks and tangled thickets of dark evergreen shrubs. Down by the water's edge was a small white house with grey shutters, the customs house. In the midst of this desolation, the government post, marked with a number like a uniform cap, had a sinister look. It was there we landed poor Palombo. A gloomy refuge for a sick man! We found the customs man about to have a meal near the fire with his wife and children. Out of their gaunt, yellow faces stared large eyes ringed with the marks of fever. The mother, still young and with a baby in her arms, was shivering as she spoke to us.

'It's a terrible place,' the inspector said softly to me. 'We have to change the customs men here every two years. The fever from the marshes eats them away . . .'

The question was, however, how to get a doctor. There was none nearer than Sartène, that is to say six or eight leagues from there. What was to be done? Our sailors could do no more; it was too far to send one of the children. Then the wife, leaning out of the door, called:

'Cecco! . . . Cecco!'

And we saw a tall, well-built young fellow enter, a typical poacher or *banditto* with his brown woollen cap and his goat-skin cloak. I had already noticed him, as we were landing, seated outside the door, a red pipe in his mouth and a gun between his knees. But he had fled – I don't know why – as we approached. Perhaps he thought we had some gendarmes with us. As he came in, the wife of the customs man blushed a little.

'He is my cousin . . .' she told us. 'No danger of him getting lost in the *maquis*.'

Then she said something to him in a low voice, pointing to the sick man. The man nodded without replying, went out, whistled to his dog, and then was gone, his gun on his shoulder, leaping with his long legs from rock to rock.

Whilst this was happening, the children, whom the presence of the inspector seemed to terrify, quickly finished their meal of chestnuts and *brucio* (white cheese). And still only water, nothing but water on the table! How good it would have been, a drop of wine, for these little ones! The misery of it all! The mother at last took them upstairs to bed; the father, lighting his lantern, went to survey the coastline, and we stayed by the fire watching our sick man who was tossing on his mean bed as if he were still far out at sea buffeted by the waves. To ease his pain a little we heated some stones and bricks and put them against his side. Once or twice, when I went over to his bed, the poor fellow recognized me and, to thank me, held out his hand painfully, a huge hand, rough and burning hot like one of those bricks just taken from the fire . . .

The night passed sadly, watching him. Outside, the bad weather had come back at night fall, and the battle of the rocks and the sea was a rumbling, roaring din of spuming foam. Now and then a blast of wind from the open sea succeeded in slipping into the bay and enveloped the house. We sensed it by the unexpected leap of the flame which suddenly lit up the mournful faces of the sailors grouped round the hearth, gazing at the fire with the imperturbable expression of those accustomed to vast expanses and far horizons. Sometimes also, Palombo moaned gently. Then all eyes turned to the dark corner where their poor friend was soon to die, far from his loved ones, without help. The watchers' chests would heave and they would give deep sighs. That was all that was wrenched from these patient gentle artisans of the sea, the feeling of their own sad lot. No thought of mutiny, of going on strike. Only a sigh, and nothing more! . . . And yet, I may be mistaken. Passing in front of me to throw some sticks on the fire, one of them said softly to me in a heart-broken voice:

'You see, monsieur . . . sometimes our job has its bad times . . .'

The Vicar of Cucugnan*

EVERY year, at Candlemas, the poets of Provence publish at Avignon an amusing little book packed with good tales and beautiful verses. This year's copy has just arrived and I've found a charming tale in verse in it which I must translate for you, shortening it a little ... So hold out your baskets, Parisians, you are going to be favoured this time with the finest flour of Provence...

Father Martin was vicar ... of Cucugnan.

He was also a man of great and simple goodness, who loved his flock at Cucugnan as a father loves his children. In his eyes, his parish at Cucugnan would have been paradise on earth if the people of Cucugnan could only have given him a little more satisfaction. But, alas, the spiders spun their webs in his confessional, and, on holy Easter Days, the Sacrament remained unneeded at the back of the ciborium. The good priest was sore at heart, and he prayed ceaselessly that by God's good grace he might not die before he had brought his scattered flock back safely to the fold.

That God heard him, you shall now see.

One Sunday, after the Gospel, Father Martin ascended into his pulpit.

'My brethren,' he said, 'whether you believe what I am going to tell you is entirely your own affair. The other night

*A fictitious place; Daudet perhaps took the name from Cucuron in Vaucluse.

I found myself, miserable sinner that I am, standing at the gates of Paradise.

'I knocked: Saint Peter opened to me.

'"Well, well! It's you, is it, good Monsieur Martin?" he said to me. "What lucky chance brings you this way? How can I be of service to you?"

'"Good Saint Peter, you who hold the key and the great book, can you tell me, if it's not asking too much, how many of the people of Cucugnan you have in Paradise?"

'"There's nothing I can refuse you, Monsieur Martin. Sit yourself down, and we'll look into the matter together."

'And Saint Peter picked up his big book, opened it and put on his spectacles.

'"Now let's see. Cucugnan, you said. Cu ... Cu ... Cucugnan. Here we are, Cucugnan. My dear Monsieur Martin, the page is quite empty. Not a soul. No more than there are fish-bones in a turkey."

'"What! No one here from Cucugnan? Nobody? It is not possible! Do look again ..."

'"Nobody, holy man. Look for yourself, if you think I'm joking."

'Then I – alas – I stamped my feet and clasped my hands and cried aloud for mercy on us all. But Saint Peter said:

'"Believe me, Monsieur Martin, you should not upset yourself in this way, for it might give you a stroke. It's not your fault, after all. Your people from Cucugnan must obviously be doing their little spell of quarantine in Purgatory."

'"Oh, good Saint Peter, for pity's sake then let me go and see them and console them."

'"Willingly, my friend ... Wait, slip on these sandals quickly, for the paths there aren't as good as they might be ... That's better ... Now follow the path straight in front of you. Then, right down there, do you see at the bottom a turning? Well, you'll find there a silver door covered all over with black crosses . . . It's on your right . . . Knock at the door and someone will open it . . . Good-bye then! Keep well and have courage!"

'And I followed that path! . . . I kept on following that path! What a tramp I had! The thought of it now makes me shudder. That narrow path, full of brambles and carbuncles that glittered and serpents that hissed, led me at last to the silver door.

'"Knock, knock!"

'"Who's knocking?" said a doleful, raucous voice.

'"The vicar of Cucugnan."

'"Of . . . ?"

'"Of Cucugnan."

'"Ah! . . . Enter."

'I entered. A great, beautiful angel, with wings dark as night, with a robe bright as day, with a diamond-studded key hanging at his waist, was writing, going scratch-scratch, in a big book more immense than Saint Peter's . . .

'"All right, what d'you want and what's your business?" said the angel.

'"Beautiful angel of God, I should like to know – though perhaps I'm being a little too curious – if you've got the people from Cucugnan here?"

'"The people from . . . ?"

'"From Cucugnan, the people from Cucugnan . . . I'm their priest, you see."

'"Ah! You're Father Martin, are you?"

'"At your service, great Angel."

'"Cucugnan, you say . . ."

'And the angel opens his book and turns over the leaves, wetting his finger to turn them quickly.

'"Cucugnan," he says, after giving a long sigh . . . "Monsieur Martin, we have nobody from Cucugnan in Purgatory."

' "Oh, Jesus, Mary and Joseph! Nobody from Cucugnan in Purgatory? Oh, dear Lord, where are they then?"

' "Why, man of God, they're in Paradise then! Where the deuce d'you want them to be?"

' "But I've just come from there, from Paradise . . ."

' "You've just come from there! Well?"

' "Well! They're not there! . . . Oh, Holy Mother of the Angels! . . ."

' "You will have to face it then, Monsieur Martin! If they're not in Paradise and not in Purgatory, there's only one other place. They're in . . ."

' "Oh, Holy Cross! Oh Jesus, Son of David! Oh, no, no, no! It isn't possible! Perhaps Saint Peter wasn't telling the truth! Perhaps he was lying . . . No, I didn't hear the cock crowing! Oh, miserable wretches we all are! How can I go to Paradise if my people of Cucugnan are not there?"

' "My poor Monsieur Martin, since you want to know the worst with your own eyes, whatever the cost, you must take that path. I advise you to run down it all the way if you can . . . On your left you will see a big gate. There you will be told everything. May God go with you!"

'And the angel closed the door.

'It was a long footpath covered all the way with glowing red-hot cinders. I staggered down it as if I'd been drinking; at every step I kept stumbling; I was soaked with perspiration, sweat was pouring off me; I kept panting and my mouth went dry with thirst . . . and yet my feet were not burnt, thanks to the sandals which the good Saint Peter had lent me.

'When I had hobbled and limped far enough, I saw on my left a door . . . no, a colossal portal, yawning wide open, like the door of an immense furnace. Oh, my brethren, what a terrible sight it was! There, nobody asked my name; there, no register is kept. No, my brethren, that door is kept wide open and people enter there in batches, just as on Sundays you go into the taverns.

'I was pouring great drops of sweat, and yet I was shivering with cold. My hair was standing on end. I smelt the burning smell of roasting flesh, a little like the smell all Cucugnan knows when old Eloy, the blacksmith, is burning the hoof of an old ass before he shoes it. I felt myself gasping for air in that burning, stinking atmosphere. I could hear the most horrible howling, loud with wailing, yelling, and with curses.

' "Well, are you coming in or aren't you?" said a demon with big horns, pricking me with his fork.

' "Me? I'm not coming in. I'm a friend of God."

' "You're a friend of God? Well, what are you doing here, you scurvy b . . . ?"

' "I've come . . . I've come . . . Bear with me a moment . . . I can hardly stand up . . . I've come . . . I've come a long way . . . to ask you . . . humbly . . . if . . . if, by any chance, . . . you have anyone here . . . anyone here from Cucugnan . . ."

' "Fires of God! Don't you try to be funny with me! As if you didn't know very well all Cucugnan is here! Look over there, you ugly crow, and you'll see what we do with your precious lot from Cucugnan! . . ."

'And I saw, in the midst of dreadful, whirling sheets of flame:

'Big Coq-Galine – you all knew him, my brethren – Coq-Galine who was always getting drunk and always beating his wife Clairon.

'I saw Catarinet . . . that little trollop . . . with her nose in the air . . . who used to sleep alone in the barn . . . you remember her all right, my fine fellows! . . . But no more about her, I've said enough.

'I saw Pascal Doigt-de-Poix, who used to make his oil from Monsieur Julien's olives.

'I saw Babet, the gleaner, who used to pull fistfuls out of the sheaves to fill her basket.

'I saw Lawyer Grapasi, who was so good at feathering his nest.

'And Dauphine, who charged so much for the water from his well.

'And Tortillard, who when he met me carrying the Sacrament to the dying, used to pass me by, with his cap on his head and his pipe in his mouth . . . proud as Lucifer . . . as if I were a dog he'd met.

'And Coulan, with his Zette, and Jacques, and Pierre, and Toni . . .'

White-faced and shaking with fear, the audience groaned at seeing within the wide-open gates of Hell, this one his father, that one his mother, another his grandmother, and still another his sister . . .

'You are well aware, my brethren,' continued the good Father Martin. 'You are well aware that this cannot go on. I am charged with the care of your souls and I must, I must, save you from the abyss into which you are about to plunge head-first. Tomorrow, I shall set to work, tomorrow at the latest. And plenty of work there will be! Here is how I shall go about it. To do the job properly, it will all have to be done in an orderly way. We will take you row by row, like when you go dancing at Jonquières.

'Tomorrow, Monday, I shall confess the old men and women. That will not take long.

'Tuesday, the infants. I shall soon be through with them.

'Wednesday, the boys and girls. That may take quite a time.

'Thursday, the men. We'll cut that as short as possible.

'Friday, the women. I'll say now: I don't want any long tales.

'Saturday, the miller! . . . He'll need a whole day to himself at least . . .

'And if we have finished by Sunday, we'll be lucky.

'You see, my children, when the corn is ripe, it has to be cut; when the wine is drawn, it has to be drunk. And when there is enough dirty linen, it has to be washed, and it has to be washed well.

'That is the grace I wish you. Amen!'

What was said was done. The dirty linen was washed.

Ever since that memorable Sunday, the sweet scent of the virtues of Cucugnan perfumes the air for ten leagues around.

And the good pastor, Father Martin, happy and light of heart, dreamed the other night that, followed in procession by all his flock and surrounded by lighted candles and clouds of incense and choir boys chanting the *Te Deum*, he was climbing the way of knowledge and light to the city of God.

Such is the story of the vicar of Cucugnan as I was commanded to tell it you by that splendid rascal Roumanille,* who had it himself from yet another good companion.

*Joseph Roumanille (1818–91), Provençal poet and short-story writer, founder of the Felibrige movement.

12

The Old Couple

'A LETTER, Azan?'

'Yes, monsieur . . . It's from Paris, monsieur.'

He was quite proud of it coming from Paris, was good old Azan . . . I wasn't. Something told me this letter from Paris, falling so unexpectedly and so early in the morning on my table, was going to rob me of my whole day. I wasn't mistaken; see for yourselves:

My dear friend, you must do me a favour. You will lock up your windmill for a day and go straight to Eyguières – the large village about three or four leagues from where you live – it's not far to walk. When you get there, you will ask for the Convent Orphanage. The first house after the Orphanage is a small one with grey shutters and a little garden behind it. You will go in without knocking – the door is always open – but you will call out very loudly: 'Good-morning, good people! I am Maurice's friend . . .' Then you will see two old people – oh, they are so very old now, my friend – and they will stretch out their arms to you from their big armchairs, and you will embrace them for me with all your heart – just as if they belonged to you. Then you will talk; they will talk about me, about nothing but me. They will tell thousands of silly things, and you will listen without laughing . . . You will not laugh, will you? They are my grandparents, the two beings to whom I mean everything in life and who have not seen me for ten years . . . Ten years is a long time! But what can I do? Paris keeps me from going to them; their great age keeps them from coming to me . . . They are so old they would collapse on the way if they came to see me. Fortunately, you are there, my dear miller, and, by embracing you they will think they are embracing me a little . . . I have written to them often about us and about our good friendship, which I . . .

To the devil with friendship! His confounded letter arrived on a beautiful morning, but such fine weather in Provence is not good for walking – too much mistral, too much sun. I had already decided upon a certain sheltered spot between two rocks and had been looking forward to remaining there all day, like a lizard, drinking in the sun and listening to the song of the pines . . . Well, what would you have done? I grumbled, locked the mill, pushed the key into the hole cut for the cat, picked up my stick and pipe, and set off.

I got to Eyguières about two o'clock. The village was deserted; everybody was in the fields. In the elm trees the cicadas were singing loudly. A donkey was sunning itself in front of the mayor's office, some pigeons were perched on the fountain outside the church, but nobody anywhere to direct me to the Orphanage. By great good luck, an old witch suddenly appeared seated at her doorstep, busy spinning. I told her what I was looking for, and since she was a very powerful old witch, she had only to lift her broom and there was the Orphanage standing before me as if by magic. It was a large, dark, forbidding place, proudly displaying an old red sandstone cross above its arched doorway, with some words in Latin around it. Next to this building, I saw a small house – with grey shutters and a little garden behind it . . . I recognized it and went in without knocking.

Always will I remember that long, quiet, cool passage, with its pink walls, the little sun-lit garden shimmering behind the thin blind at the far end, and the faded flowers and the violins on the panels of the wainscoting. It was as if I had entered the home of some old bailiff in a play by Sedaine. At the end of the passage, on the left through a half-open door, I could hear the tick-tock of a large clock, and a child's voice reading aloud, as they do at school, stopping after each syllable: THEN ... SAINT ... IR ... EN ... EUS ... CRIED ... OUT ... I ... AM ... THE ... WHEAT ... OF ... THE. .LORD ... IT ... IS ... NEC ... ESS ... ARY ... THAT ... I ... BE ... GROUND ... BY ... THE ... TEETH ... OF ... THESE ... AN ... I ... MALS ... I approached the door softly and looked in ...

In the stillness and the subdued light of a small room a kindly looking old man, rosy-cheeked and wrinkled to his finger-tips, was fast asleep in a deep armchair, his mouth open, his hands resting on his knees. At his feet a little girl dressed in blue – a little hood and a long cape, the uniform of the Orphanage – was reading the life of Saint Ireneus out of a book bigger than herself ...

This tale of miracles had performed a miracle upon the whole house. All slept: the old man in his armchair, the flies on the ceiling, the canaries in their cage over there on the window-sill. The big clock snored, tick-tock, tick-tock. Nothing remained awake in all the room except a broad ray of sunlight which shone between the closed shutters, a straight, white beam, full of living sparks and microscopic waltzes ... Amidst this general slumber, the child gravely went on with her reading: STRAIGHT ... WAY ... TWO ... LIONS ... FELL ... UP ... ON ... HIM ... AND ... DE ... VOURED ... HIM ... It was at this point that I entered ... The results were dramatic! If the lions of Saint Ireneus themselves had leapt into the room they could not have caused more astonishment. The little girl shrieked, the big book dropped, the canaries and flies awoke, the clock struck, the old man jumped up shaking with fright, and I myself, a little uneasy, stopped short on the threshold where I called out, very loudly:

'Good-day, good people! I am Maurice's friend.'

Oh, if you only could have seen the poor old man then!

If you could have seen him come to me with open arms, embrace me, shake my hands, run bewildered round the room exclaiming:

'Oh, good gracious me! Oh, good gracious me!'

His face had gone quite red and every wrinkle in it was laughing. He kept stammering:

'Oh, monsieur! . . . Oh, monsieur! . . .'

Then he went to the back of the room and called:

'Mamette!'

The sound of a door opening and a mouse-like pattering in the passage. It was Mamette: a dear little old woman in a beribboned bonnet and a Carmelite gown, and holding in her hand an embroidered handkerchief to do me honour, as was the fashion long ago. It touched me greatly to see how much they resembled each other! With some ribbons and bows his name also could have been Mamette. But the real Mamette must have shed many tears in her life, because she had even more wrinkles than he. Like him, too, she was attended by a child from the Orphanage, a little guardian in a blue cape who never left her. And to see those two old people watched over by these orphan children was more moving than anything I could ever have imagined. As she came in, Mamette had started to make me a low curtsey, but it was quickly cut short as soon as the old man said:

'This is Maurice's friend . . .'

She trembles, weeps, loses her handkerchief, flushes an even deeper red than he. These old people, they've only a drop of blood in their veins, and the least agitation sends it rushing to their faces . . .

'Quick, quick, a chair . . .' says the old woman to her little girl.

'Open the shutters . . .' cries the old man to his.

And, taking me each by a hand, they lead me at a trot to the now wide-open window in order to get a better look at me. Then the armchairs are pushed forward, I sit down between them on a stool, the little girls in blue behind us, and the interrogation begins:

'How is he? What is he doing? Why doesn't he come? Is he happy?'

And so on and so on like that, for hours.

I did my best to answer all their questions, giving what details I knew about my friend, shamelessly inventing those I did not know, taking special care not to confess I had never noticed if his windows shut tight, or even the colour of his wall-paper.

'His wall-paper! . . . It's blue, madame, light blue with a garland design.'

'Really?' exclaimed the old lady with great emotion, and added, turning to her husband: 'He's such a good boy!'

'Indeed he is! A fine lad!' the old man replied enthusiastically.

And all the time I was speaking, they kept nodding their heads at each other, giving little laughs, and winking in a knowing way at each other. But, sometimes, the old man would lean towards me and say:

'Speak louder! . . . She doesn't hear too well!'

Then she, in her turn:

'A little louder, I beg you! . . . His hearing is not too good.'

So I would raise my voice, and both of them would thank me with a smile. And they would lean forward as if seeking within my eyes some image of their Maurice. It was then that I found myself most deeply moved; for in those tired smiles of theirs, I seemed myself to see the image of my friend, elusive, vague, dim, as though he were smiling at me himself from far away through a deep mist.

Suddenly the old man sits up in his chair.

'Mamette, I've just thought . . . perhaps he has not had any lunch!'

And Mamette raises her hands in consternation.

'Not had any lunch! Oh, gracious me!'

I thought they were still going on about Maurice, and was about to say that the dear lad always made sure he lunched by midday. But not a bit of it; it was myself they were talking about. And you should have seen the fuss when I admitted that I had not eaten.

'Quick, little blue ones, lay the table! Move it to the middle of the room; the Sunday cloth, the flowered plates! Quickly now, and do not laugh so much, please!'

And they were quick! They'd only time to break three plates and lunch was served!

'Now it's a good little lunch!' said Mamette as she led me to the table. 'But you'll have to eat alone. We had ours this morning.'

These old people! Whatever time you call on them, they've always had a meal that morning!

Mamette's good little lunch consisted of two fingers of milk, some dates, and a *barquette*, a sort of sweet-bread enough to feed her and her canaries for at least a week . . . And I managed it all by myself! The indignation there must have been around that table! How the little blue ones must have whispered and nudged each other! How the canaries over in their cage must have seemed to be saying: 'Oh, just look! That gentleman is eating all the *barquette*!'

I did indeed eat it all, almost without realizing it, so absorbed was I in looking round that bright room, so peaceful, so redolent of times long past . . . In particular – I could not take my eyes away from them – there were two little beds. I kept picturing those little beds – almost cradles – each morning at dawn, both still hidden behind their long, fringed curtains. Three o'clock strikes. It is the hour when all old folk find themselves awake.

'Are you asleep, Mamette?'

'No, my dear.'

'Maurice is a good boy, isn't he?'

'He is indeed! A fine lad!'

And I imagined a whole conversation like that, just from seeing those two old people's little beds, standing side by side.

Meanwhile, a terrible drama was taking place in front of the cupboard at the other end of the room. It concerned how exactly to reach, high up on the top shelf, a certain jar of cherries in brandy which had been waiting for Maurice for ten years and which they wished to open for me. In spite of Mamette's pleas, the old man had insisted on getting the cherries himself, and having climbed on to a chair, was trying to reach up for them, to the horrified dismay of his wife . . . You can imagine the scene: the old man reaching up unsteadily, the little blue ones grasping his chair tightly, Mamette behind him holding her breath, her arms outstretched, and all of them enveloped in the faint perfume of bergamot from the open cupboard and its big piles of unbleached linen . . . I watched entranced.

At last, after prodigious efforts, they succeeded in getting that famous jar down from the cupboard, and with it an old battered silver mug, the mug that Maurice had used when a child. They filled it for me to the brim with cherries; Maurice so much liked cherries! And whilst he was serving me, the old man kept whispering in my ear, as though he fancied them himself:

'You are very lucky, you know! To be able to eat them! My wife bottled them! They're good – you see!'

Alas, his wife had bottled them but she'd forgotten to sweeten them. But old people become absent-minded; it was what one could have expected. Your cherries were atrocious, my poor Mamette . . . but that did not stop me eating every single one of them – without batting one eyelid.

The meal over, I got up to say good-bye to my hosts.

They'd have much liked to keep me a little longer to talk about their dear boy, but the day was drawing to its close and the mill was far away; I had to go.

The old man had risen with me.

'Mamette, my coat! . . . I'm going to take him as far as the square.'

I'm quite certain Mamette really thought it was already too chilly for him to go as far as the square, but she also did not bat an eyelid. Only, when she was helping him get his arms into the sleeves of his coat, a fine, snuff-coloured coat with mother-of-pearl buttons, I heard her say softly to him:

'You won't be back too late, will you?'

And he, with a roguish air:

'Ho, ho! How should I know! . . . Perhaps! . . .'

On which, they looked at each other and laughed, and the little blue ones laughed to see them laugh, and over in their corner the canaries in their own way laughed also. Between you and me, I think the smell of the cherries had gone a little to the heads of all of them.

. . . As grandfather and I went out, night was falling. His little blue one followed us at a distance, to take him back again; but he did not see her, and it obviously gave him great pride to walk with his arm in mine, like a man. Mamette, her face all smiles, watched this from her doorstep, and, as she followed us with her eyes, she kept nodding her little head in delight as if to say: 'There, you see! He can still walk, that poor man of mine!'

13

Ballads in Prose

WHEN I opened my door this morning I found my mill
surrounded by a great carpet of white frost. The grass was
glittering and crackling like glass; all the hill was shivering
. . . For one day my dear Provence had disguised itself as a
northern country; and it is among pines edged with hoar-
frost and tufts of lavender transformed into sprays of crystal
that I have written these two ballads with their slight flavour
of teutonic fantasy, whilst all around me the frost was
sprinkling its sparkling, white tinsel, and far above, in the
clear sky, great triangles of storks from the land of the poet
Heine were flying towards the Camargue crying: 'It is
cold . . . cold . . .'

1. *The Death of the Dauphin*

The little Dauphin is ill, the little Dauphin is going to
die . . . In all the churches of the Kingdom, the Holy Sacrament remains on view night and day, and tall candles are
burning for the recovery of the royal child. The streets
around the royal residence are silent and sad, the bells no
longer sound, the carriages move at a walking pace . . . At
the approaches to the palace, curious citizens gaze through
the railings at the golden-stomached Swiss Guards, talking
in the courtyards with an air of importance. The whole
palace is in a state of confusion. Chamberlains and majordomos run up and down the marble stairs . . . The galleries
are crowded with pages and courtiers attired in silks, all
moving from one group to the next, asking in whispers for

the latest news ... On the wide steps, weeping maids of honour make low curtseys to one another, as they wipe their eyes with pretty, embroidered handkerchiefs.

In the Orangery, there is a numerous conclave of robed physicians. They can be seen through the windows, waving their long, black sleeves, and nodding learnedly their big-wigged heads. Outside the door, the little Dauphin's Tutor and his Equerry are walking up and down awaiting the decision of the Medical Faculty. Kitchen scullions pass close to them without making any salutation. Monsieur the Equerry is swearing like a trooper; Monsieur the Tutor is reciting lines from Horace ... And, all the while, from down there in the direction of the stables, a loud plaintive neighing can be heard. It is the little Dauphin's chestnut horse whom the grooms have forgotten and who is calling sadly from beside his empty manger.

And the King? Where is His Majesty the King? His Majesty has shut himself up all alone in a room at the far end of the palace ... Kings do not like their tears to be seen ... With the Queen, it is a different matter ... She is sitting beside the little Dauphin's bed, her lovely face wet with tears, sobbing aloud in front of everyone, just like any draper's wife would.

In his little lace-trimmed bed, the little Dauphin, paler than the pillows beneath his head, is lying still. Though the little body lies straight and his eyes are closed, he is not sleeping ... He turns his head towards his mother and sees that she is weeping. He says:

'Madame, why are you weeping? Is it because you really believe I am going to die?'

The Queen tries to reply. Her sobs overwhelm her.

'Then do not weep, Madame. You forget that I am the Dauphin and that Dauphins cannot die in this way ...'

The Queen sobs louder than ever, and the little Dauphin begins to be afraid.

'You all there, hear me!' he says. 'It is not my wish that Death should come and take me like this, and I know full well how to stop him entering here ... Summon at once forty of the strongest soldiers to mount guard around my bed! ... Let one hundred cannon keep watch night and day, their linstocks lit ready, beneath my windows! If then Death dare come near me, it will be all the worse for him!'

To humour the royal child, the Queen makes a sign. In no time, huge cannon can be heard rolling into the court-yard, and forty tall soldiers, halberds in hand, enter and range themselves around the room. They are all old, grey-moustached veterans. The little Dauphin claps his hands as he sees them. He recognizes one, and calls to him:

'Lorrain! Lorrain!'

The old soldier takes one step forward.

'I like you very much, old Lorrain ... Do just let me see your sword ... If Death tries to take me, it will be necessary to kill him, won't it?'

Lorrain answers:

'Yes, your Highness.'

And two big tears roll down his weather-beaten cheeks. Just then, the Chaplain draws close to the little Dauphin, whispers a long time to him, showing him a crucifix. The little Dauphin listens to him with a look of astonishment, then suddenly interrupts:

'Yes, I understand all you say, monsieur, but, really, wouldn't it be possible for my friend Beppo to die instead of me, if we give him a lot of money ? . . .'

The Chaplain continues to whisper to him, and the little Dauphin looks more and more astonished.

When the Chaplain has finished the little Dauphin sighs deeply and answers:

'All you have just told me, monsieur, is very sad; but one thing comforts me and that is that up there in Paradise, up among the stars, I shall still be the Dauphin. I know that God is my cousin and He cannot fail to receive me according to my rank.'

Then, turning to his mother, he adds:

'Have my finest clothes brought here, my white ermine doublet and my velvet shoes! I want to look my best in front of the angels and to enter Paradise in clothes befitting the Dauphin.'

For the third time, the Chaplain bends down to the little Dauphin and whispers to him for a long time . . . At last the royal child interrupts him, crying out angrily:

'But then, to be Dauphin means nothing at all!'

And, refusing to listen anymore, the little Dauphin turns his face to the wall, and cries bitterly.

II. *The Sub-Prefect is Confused*

Monsieur the Sub-Prefect is on his rounds. Coachman in front, lackey behind, the Sub-Prefecture carriage is conveying him majestically to the district agricultural show at La Combe-aux-Fées. For this memorable outing, Monsieur the Sub-Prefect has put on his fine, embroidered coat, his little cocked hat, his tight-fitting, silver-braided breeches and his best sword with the mother-of-pearl hilt . . . On his knees rests a large portfolio of embossed leather. He gazes at it sourly.

The Sub-Prefect's look is sour as he gazes at his embossed leather portfolio because he is thinking of the important speech he will shortly have to deliver to the inhabitants of the Combe-Aux-Fées:

'Gentlemen – whom it is my good fortune to have under my jurisdiction . . .'

But no matter how much he twists and twirls his side-whiskers and how many times he repeats:

'Gentlemen . . . my good fortune . . . under my juris-diction . . .' his speech gets no further.

His speech gets no further . . . It's so hot in this carriage! As far ahead as he can see, the dusty road to La Combe-aux-Fées stretches under the burning sun of the Midi . . . The air is like a furnace . . . and on the elms, covered with white dust, which line the road thousands of cicadas chatter back and forth from tree to tree. Suddenly Monsieur the Sub-Prefect gives a start. In the distance, at the foot of a low hill, he has just seen a little wood of evergreen oak trees, and it seems as if it is beckoning to him.

The little wood of evergreen oaks seems to be saying:

'Do come over here to prepare your speech, Monsieur the Sub-Prefect. You will feel much better under my trees . . .'

The Sub-Prefect cannot resist; he jumps down from his carriage, telling his servants to wait for him; that he is going to compose his speech in the little wood of evergreen oaks.

In the little wood of evergreen oaks there are birds and violets and springs of water hidden trickling under the grass . . . When they caught sight of Monsieur the Sub-Prefect, in his fine knee-breeches and with his embossed leather portfolio, the birds were frightened and stopped singing, the springs of water did not dare make another sound, and the violets hid themselves in the grass ... All their little world had never seen a Sub-Prefect, and they asked each other in whispers who this fine gentleman might be who walked about in silver breeches.

In whispers, beneath the leaves, they ask each other who this fine gentleman in silver breeches may be ... Meanwhile, the Sub-Prefect, delighted with the silence and the coolness of the wood, tucks up his coat-tails, lays his cocked hat on the grass and seats himself on the moss at the foot of a young oak. Then he rests his portfolio of embossed leather on his knees, opens it, and takes out a wide sheet of official paper.

'He's an artist!' says the warbler.

'No,' says the bullfinch, 'he's not an artist because he's got silver breeches. He's more likely a prince.'

'He's more likely a prince,' says the bullfinch.

'Not an artist nor a prince,' interrupts an old nightingale, who had sung in the gardens of the Sub-Prefecture ... 'I know who he is. He is a Sub-Prefect!'

And all the little wood begins to whisper:

'He's a Sub-Prefect! He's a Sub-Prefect!'

'How bald he is!' observes a lark who has a great crest on his head.

The violets ask:

'Is he dangerous?'

'Is he dangerous?' the violets ask.

The old nightingale replies:

'By no means!'

And, on this assurance, the birds begin to sing again, the springs of water to flow, and the sweet violets to scent the air, just as if the gentleman were not there ...

Undisturbed by all this jocund uproar, the Sub-Prefect is fervently invoking the Muse that protects agricultural shows, and, pencil raised, begins to declaim pompously:

'Gentlemen – whom it is my good fortune to have under my jurisdiction . . .'

'Gentlemen – whom it is my good fortune to have under my jurisdiction,' declaims the Sub-Prefect pompously . . .

A peal of laughter interrupts him. He turns round and sees nothing but a big woodpecker perched on his cocked hat looking at him, and laughing. The Sub-Prefect shrugs his shoulders and is about to continue with his speech when the woodpecker interrupts him again, shouting at him this time from farther off:

'What's the point of it all?'

'What d'you mean? What's the point of it all?' says the Sub-Prefect, getting red in the face; and, shooing away the impertinent creature with a wave of his arm, he begins again, even more pompously:

'Gentlemen – whom it is my good fortune to have under my jurisdiction . . .'

'Gentlemen – whom it is my good fortune to have under my jurisdiction . . .' began the Sub-Prefect again, even more pompously.

But then all the little violets bend on their stalks towards him and say softly:

'Monsieur the Sub-Prefect, can't you smell how sweet we smell?'

And the springs of water under the moss make celestial music; and in the branches overhead flocks of warblers come and sing to him their loveliest melodies; and all the little wood conspires to prevent him composing his speech.

All the little wood conspires to prevent him composing his speech . . . Monsieur the Sub-Prefect, intoxicated by the scents, drunk with the music tries in vain to resist the strange spell which he feels being put upon him. He unbuttons his fine coat, leans on his elbows on the grass, mutters again two or three times:

'Gentlemen . . . my good . . . under my jurisdiction . . .'

Then he sends the gentlemen under his jurisdiction to the devil; and the Muse who protects agricultural shows can only hide her face in shame.

Hide thy face, O Muse of agricultural shows! . . . For when, an hour later, the Sub-Prefect's servants, anxious about their master, came into the little wood, they saw a sight which made them draw back in horror . . . Monsieur the Sub-Prefect was lying flat on his stomach in the grass, his waistcoat undone, his coat flung down beside him, just as if he were a tramp . . . And, murmuring to himself about violets, the Sub-Prefect was composing poetry.

14

Bixiou's* Wallet

ONE morning, in the month of October, a few days before leaving Paris, there came into my room – whilst I was having breakfast – a bent and bowed old man, dirty, in worn clothes, shivering on his long legs like a plucked stork. It was Bixiou. Yes, my Parisian friends, your Bixiou, the wild and charming Bixiou, that outrageous mocker who for fifteen years delighted you so vastly with his scurrilous pamphlets and his caricatures . . . Ah, what a heart-rending sight the poor fellow was! But for the wry face he pulled as he came in, I would never have recognized him.

With his head bent towards his shoulder and his cane

*A fictitious name, though probably Daudet had in mind some actual caricaturist.

held to his teeth like a clarinet, this most famous of gloomy jesters advanced to the middle of the room, supported himself sideways against the table, and said in a doleful voice:

'Have pity on a blind man!'

It was so well imitated I couldn't help laughing. But he, he only said tonelessly:

'You believe I am joking . . . look at my eyes.'

And he turned towards me two large white pupils, sightless.

'I'm blind, my dear fellow, blind for the rest of my life. That's what came of writing with vitriol. I burnt my eyes out at that wretched job – see, burnt out . . . right to the sockets,' he added, showing me his calcined lids on which not an eyelash remained.

I was so affected I could think of nothing to say. My silence troubled him.

'You're working?'

'No, Bixiou, I am having breakfast. Would you like to join me?'

He did not reply but I saw all right from a quivering of his nostrils he was dying to say yes. I took him by the hand and sat him down near me.

While he was being served, the poor devil sniffed at the food, giving a little laugh:

'Smells goods, that does. I'm going to tuck in to this, all right. Haven't been bothering about breakfast myself for some time now! Just a bread roll every morning on my way round the Ministries . . . I'm doing a tour of the Ministries at the moment, you know. Making quite a profession of it. I'm trying to get a tobacco licence. Well, you know how it is! A home isn't much good without food. I can't sketch any more. Nor write . . . I could dictate? . . . Dictate what? I never had anything in *my* head. No imagination. The only thing I was good at was observing people, watching the expression on their faces and then sketching it. Present circumstances don't make that possible any longer . . . So I thought of a tobacconist's shop, not on the boulevards, of course. Not being the mother of a ballet dancer or the widow of a high-ranking officer, I can't ask favours like that. No, just a small tobacconist's shop in the provinces, some-where a good way off, in a corner of the Vosges perhaps. I'll stock a first-class porcelain pipe. Yes, and I'll call myself Hans or Zebediah, like in Erckmann-Chatrian, and console myself for not writing any more by making paper tobacco bags out of the writings of my colleagues.

'That's all I ask. Not much, is it? . . . All the same, it's the devil to get . . . Still, there must be people who can help. I used to dine with the General, the Prince, the Ministers; the lot of them used to invite me because I amused them or because they feared me. Now I no longer make anyone fear me. My eyes! Oh, my poor eyes! And I'm invited out no-where now. A blind man at your dinner table – so depressing you know. The swine! They intend to make me pay dearly for this miserable tobacconist's shop. For six months I've been hawking my petition from one Ministry to another. I'm there every morning just as they're lighting the stoves and taking his Excellency's horses to be exercised in the sand on the yard. I don't get away at night until the big lamps are brought in and the kitchens are beginning to smell good . . .

'All my life is passing away sitting on wooden benches in waiting rooms. Even the ushers know me by sight. It's true! At the Ministry of the Interior they call me "That nice old fellow!" And I crack jokes to get in their good books, or sketch a big moustache on the corner of their blotting paper with one stroke of my pen. That's always good for a laugh. Yes, this is what I've come to after twenty years of rip-roaring success – this is where the artistic life gets you in the end! And they say there are forty thousand young loafers with their mouths watering to get into our profession! They say trains come up from the provinces every day loaded

with fools yearning for the literary life and literary fame! . . .
Oh, romantic provinces, if only you could learn from
Bixiou's misery!'

Thereupon he thrust his nose to his plate and began to eat
greedily, not saying another word . . . It was most pitiful to
see how he managed. Every minute he would lose his bread
or his fork, or would grope for his glass. Poor fellow! He
hadn't got used to it yet.

Soon he started again:

'Do you know what's even more terrible for me? Not
being able to read the newspapers. You've got to be in our
profession to understand that . . . Sometimes on my way
home in the evening, I buy one – just to get that smell of
damp paper and fresh news print. It's so good! And nobody
to read them to me! My wife could all right, but she won't.
She makes out that some of the news items in the miscel-
laneous column aren't respectable . . . These old mistresses,
once they're married they become real old prudes. Since I
made mine Madame Bixiou, she's felt obliged to become
religious – takes it to extremes! . . . She actually wanted me
to rub my eyes with water from the Salette!* After that,
consecrated bread, collections for the conversion of Chinese
children, and heaven knows what else . . . we're up to our
necks with good works . . . It would be a good work all the
same to read me my newspapers. But no, she doesn't want
to . . . If my daughter were at home, she'd read them to me
soon enough. But when I went blind I sent her away to
Notre-Dames-des-Arts – to have a mouth less to feed . . .

'That's another one who gives me joy! Not nine years old
yet and she's had every illness going . . . And miserable! . . .
And ugly! . . . More ugly than me – if that's possible . . . A

---

*The stream at the village of that name in Isère where the Virgin
is believed to have appeared to two children. The water of the stream
is supposed to cure all diseases.

monster! But what can you expect? It's the only thing I've been any good at – creating caricatures ... But I'm a fine one boring you with my domestic troubles. They're no concern of yours. Come, give me a little more brandy. I must face up to things. When I leave you I'm going to the Ministry of Education, and the ushers there don't laugh easily. They're all old teachers.'

I poured him his brandy. He began to savour it in little sips, lingering pitifully over it. Suddenly, seized by I don't know what fancy, he stood up, glass in hand, moved his venomous blind head slowly from one direction to the other with the gracious smile of a gentleman about to make a speech, then, in a shrill voice, as if haranguing a banquet of two hundred guests:

'To the Arts! To Literature! To the Press!'

And he was off on a ten minutes' toast, the maddest and the most marvellous improvisation which had probably ever emerged from that clownish brain.

Imagine a New Year's theatrical review with the title: 'Literary Paris Today' ... our so-called literary societies, our tittle-tattle, our quarrels, all the oddities of a grotesque world, an inky dung-heap, a splendourless hell, where everybody cuts each other's throats, tears out each other's guts, picks each other's pockets, is out to get what he can as much as any self-interested capitalist and yet is more likely to die of hunger than anyone else; all our despicableness, all our shabbiness; old Baron L— of Lottery, with his wooden bowl and his pimp's coat, going off to the Tuileries Gardens to beg ... 'nyee – nyee – nyee —' then our dear departed ones, the funerals aimed at posthumous publicity, the burial oration given by our local Deputy, always the same: 'Our dear friend, so beloved and so greatly missed!' about a poor wretch for whom all of us refused to pay the cost of a tombstone; and those who have committed suicide, and those who have gone mad; imagine to yourself all that spat out, detailed, gesticulated by a mountebank of genius, and you will have an idea of Bixiou's gift of improvisation.

His toast finished, his glass empty, he asked me the time and went off, with an aggressive air, without saying good-bye ... I don't know how the ushers at the Ministry of Education enjoyed his visit that morning, but I do know that never in my life have I felt so depressed, so at odds with myself, than after the departure of that terrible blind man. My inkwell sickened me, my pen horrified me. I should have liked to go away, far away, to run, see green trees, smell something good. What hatred! What bile! What compulsion to besmirch all, to defile all! Oh, the despicable wretch! ...

And I stormed up and down my room, believing I still heard the sneering laugh of disgust he had given while talking about his daughter.

All at once, near the chair where the blind man had sat, I felt something under my feet. Bending down, I recognized his wallet, a huge shiny wallet, with frayed corners, which he is never without and which he jokingly calls his 'sack of venom'. It was as famous in our world as Monsieur de Girardin's notorious filing cases. Everybody said there were terrible things in it ... and the chance was too good to miss. The wallet, too full, had burst open when it fell and all the papers had fallen out on to the carpet. I had no alternative but to pick them up one by one ...

A bundle of letters written on paper bordered with flowers, all beginning 'My dear daddy' and signed: 'Céline Bixiou, of the Children of Mary.'

Old prescriptions for children's illnesses, croup, convulsions, scarlet fever, measles ... (the poor child hadn't escaped one!).

Last of all, a large sealed envelope from which protruded as if from under a little girl's bonnet, two or three locks of fair curly hair; in large wavering letters, the handwriting of a blind man:

Céline's hair cut on 13 May, the day she went to that place.

Now you know what there was in Bixiou's wallet.
Yes, Parisians, you are all the same. Disgust, irony, devilish laughs, vicious jokes, and then to cap them all: . . .

Céline's hair cut on 13 May.

15

The Fable of the Man with the Golden Brain

To the Lady who asks for light-hearted stories

WHEN I read your letter, madam, I had a twinge of something like remorse. I blamed myself for the sombre hue of my stories, and promised myself I would offer you something joyful today, something light-heartedly joyful.

After all, why should I be sad? I live a thousand leagues from Paris, on a sun-soaked hill, in the country of tambourines and muscat wine. Around me all is sunshine and music. I have orchestras of wheatears and choirs of tomtits. In the morning the curlews call. In the afternoon, the cicadas. Then the herdsmen come, playing the fife, and the beautiful, dark-haired girls who can be heard laughing among the vines.

In truth, the place is the least conducive to melancholy. I ought rather to be dispatching rose-coloured poems and basketfuls of love stories.

Alas, no! I am still too near to Paris. Every day, even among my pine trees, the murky splashes of her miseries reach me. At the very moment that I am writing this, I have just learnt of the miserable death of poor Charles Barbara;* and my mill is in deep mourning. Farewell, curlews and cicadas! I have heart no more for anything light and gay. That is why, madam, instead of the merry little tale I had

*A now forgotten French novelist. The reference dates this story exactly since Barbara died on 19 September 1866.

proposed to give you, you will today receive once again a melancholy fable.

Once upon a time there was a man who had a brain of gold. Yes, madam, a brain of pure gold. When he was born, the doctors thought he would not live, so heavy was his head and so enormous his skull. But live he did, and grew in the sunshine like a healthy young olive tree. His huge head, however, was always getting him into difficulties. It was pitiful to see him bumping into the furniture as he walked about. He fell over often. One day he rolled right down a flight of stairs, knocked his forehead against a marble step, and his skull rang like an ingot. They thought he was dead, but, on picking him up, only a slight cut was found, with two or three little drops of gold clotted in his fair hair. It was thus his parents learnt that the child had a brain of gold.

The matter was kept secret; the poor little boy himself suspected nothing. From time to time, he would ask why they no longer allowed him to run about in the street in front of the house with the other boys.

'You would be stolen, my treasure!' his mother would reply.

Then the child became very frightened of being stolen. He used to stay inside, playing all alone, saying nothing, dragging himself from one room to another.

Not until he was eighteen did his parents reveal to him the monstrous gift he had received from fate. And as they had fed and clothed and cared for him to that age, they asked him in return for a little of his gold. The boy did not hesitate; the very same moment – how and by what means the fable does not tell – he plucked out of his skull a piece of solid gold, as big as a walnut, and threw it proudly into his mother's lap. Then, quite dazzled by the riches he carried in his head, mad with ambitions, drunk with his power, he left his father's house and went out into the world squandering his treasure.

At the rate he lived, royally and recklessly, his treasure might have been thought inexhaustible. But exhaustible it was, and gradually his eyes were seen to become duller and his cheeks hollower. One day at last, the morning after a night of senseless debauchery, the wretched youth, left alone among the wreckage of the banquet and the fading light of the chandeliers, was struck with panic at the tremendous breach he had already made in his ingot of gold. It was time to stop.

From that moment he began a new life. The man with the brain of gold went away to live alone and by the work of his hands, suspicious and fearful like a miser, out of reach of temptations, trying to make himself forget those fateful riches which he no longer wished to use . . . Unfortunately a friend had followed him into his solitude, and this friend knew his secret.

One night the poor man was suddenly awakened with a pain, an excruciating pain, in his head. He jumped up distracted and by the light of the moon he saw the friend running away hiding something under his cloak . . .

A little more of his brain had been taken from him! . . .

Some time after that, the man with the golden brain fell in love, and this time all was over. With all his heart, he loved a little fair-haired girl who loved him also, but who loved even more frilly dresses, white feathers, and pretty bronze tassels around her little shoes.

In the hands of this dainty creature – half bird, half doll – it was a pleasure to see the pieces of gold melt away. She was full of caprice, and he could deny her nothing. For fear of upsetting her, he even to the very end hid from her the sad secret of his wealth.

'We are *very* rich, then?' she used to say.

And the poor man would reply,

'Oh, yes . . . yes, very rich!'

And he would smile with love at the little blue bird that was innocently eating his brain. But, sometimes, fear overwhelmed him and he tried to spend less. Yet then his little wife would come hopping up to him, saying,

'My rich, rich husband! Buy me something very expensive!'

And he would buy her something very expensive.

This went on for two years. Then, one morning, his little wife died, without any apparent cause, just like a bird . . . The treasure was nearly exhausted; with what he had left the widower arranged a beautiful funeral for his beloved one. A full peal of bells, heavy coaches draped with black, plumed horses, tears embroidered in silver on the black velvet hangings – nothing was too fine for her. What did his gold matter to him now? He gave it to the church, to the pall-bearers, to the women who provided the wreaths. He gave it everywhere heedlessly. So, when he left the cemetery, almost nothing remained of that marvellous brain, scarcely a few grains on the lining of the brain-pan.

Then he was seen wandering the streets distractedly, groping his way with his hands, staggering like a drunkard. In the evening, when the shops were lighting up, he stopped in front of a shop-window filled with a jumble of fabrics and finery glistening in the lights, and remained there for a long time, looking at two little blue satin boots lined with swan's down. 'I know someone to whom those little boots would give a lot of pleasure,' he said to himself, smiling. And no longer even remembering that his little wife was dead, he went in to buy them.

The shop-keeper, in the back room of her shop, heard a great cry. She ran in and drew back with fear on seeing a man leaning sideways against the counter, staring at her as if in terrible pain. He was grasping in one hand the little blue boots lined with swan's down, and holding out to her his other hand, all covered with blood but with scrapings of gold on his finger-nails.

Such, madam, is the fable of the man with the brain of gold.

Although it sounds an unbelievable story, this fable is true from beginning to end. There are in this world un- fortunate people who are condemned to live by their brain and who pay in fine gold, with their marrow and their very substance, for the least things in life. For them, life is a daily renewal of pain; and then, when they are weary of suffering . . .

16

The Poet Mistral

WHEN I got up on Sunday morning, I thought I had awoken in the rue du Faubourg – Montmartre. It was raining, the sky was grey, the mill depressing. The thought of spending this cold, wet day by myself scared me, and suddenly I found myself wanting to go and find again the warmth I've always found in the company of Frédéric Mistral, the great poet who lives three leagues from my pines, in the little village of Maillane.

No sooner thought than done: a staff of myrtle wood, my Montaigne, a blanket, and I was off!

Nobody in the fields ... Our lovely Provence, being Catholic, allows the soil to rest on Sundays ... The farm-houses are shut up, only the dogs are at home ... Now and then, I meet a carrier's cart, its tarpaulin streaming with water; an old woman muffled in a mantle the colour of dead leaves; mules, in blue and white holiday finery with red pompoms and silver bells, pulling at a trot a light cart full of farm folk on their way to Mass; and, down below, through the mist, I see a boat on the canal and a fisherman standing in it casting his net.

Not a day for reading on the way. The rain was falling in torrents and the tramontane hurled it in bucketsful into my face . . . I did the journey without a stop, and at last, after walking for three hours, I saw in front of me the little cypress woods in which the village of Maillane shelters from the wind.

Not a soul about in the village streets; all were at High Mass. As I passed the church the wind-instruments were booming and I could see the light of the candles through the coloured windows.

The poet's home is at the end of the village, the last house on the left, on the road to Saint-Remy. It is small, only one storey, with a garden in front of it . . . I go in quietly . . . Nobody there! The sitting-room door is closed, but behind it I hear someone walking up and down, speaking in a loud voice: it is a step and a voice I know well. I pause a moment, very excited, in the little white-washed passage, with my hand on the door knob. My heart beats faster. He is there! Had I better wait until he has finished the verse? . . . No, I shall risk it! I shall go in.

Ah, Parisians, when the poet of Maillane came to Paris to show you his *Mireille*, and when you saw him in your drawing-rooms this Chactas* in town clothes, with a stiff collar and a big hat which made him feel as uncomfortable as his fame did, you thought that was Mistral . . . No, that was not he. In all this world there is only one Mistral: he whom

*A Red Indian chief in Chateaubriand's novel *Les Natchez* which gives an account of his visit to France.

I surprised in his village last Sunday, his little felt cap over one ear, no waistcoat beneath his jacket, but around his waist the red Catalan sash, his eyes shining with the inspiration of his genius, a warm smile on his superb face, graceful as a Greek god, striding up and down with his hands in his pockets, making poetry . . .

'It's you! This *is* a surprise!' Mistral cries, and throws his arms around me, 'What a wonderful idea to come and see me! Especially today – it's the feast-day in Maillane. We've a band from Avignon, bulls, a procession, the farandole, it's all going to be magnificent . . . My mother will be back soon from Mass; we'll have lunch – and then out we'll go to have a look at the pretty girls dancing . . .'

While he was speaking, I looked with emotion around this little room, hung with light tapestry, which I had not seen for so long and where I had spent so many happy hours. Nothing had changed. The sofa was still there with its yellow-check cover, the two straw-seated armchairs, the armless Venus and the Venus of Arles on the mantelpiece, the poet's portrait by Hébert, his photograph by Etienne Carjat, and, in a corner by the window, his desk – an ordinary little table such as you see in registry offices, piled high with books and dictionaries. In the middle of the desk I saw a thick notebook lying open. It was *Calendal*, Frédéric Mistral's new poem, which is to be published at the end of this year, on Christmas Day. Mistral worked on this poem for seven years and it is six months since he wrote the last stanza, yet he cannot bring himself to leave it. There is always, you see, a stanza in need of polishing, a more resonant rhyme to be sought. Even though Mistral writes in the language of Provence, he works over his verses as if all the world were going to be able to read them in the original and call him to account for his workmanship. What a poet! It could indeed have been of Mistral that Montaigne wrote: 'Remember the man who, when asked why he took so much trouble over an art which so few people would appreciate, replied: "It is enough for me if there are but few. It is enough for me if there is but one. It is enough for me if there is not even one." '

I was holding in my hands the notebook in which Mistral wrote *Calendal*, and was turning its pages, deeply moved . . . All at once, the music of fifes and drums is heard in the street beneath the window, and behold Mistral runs to the cupboard, takes out glasses, bottles, pulls the table to the middle of the room, and flings open the door to the musicians, saying to me:

'Don't laugh . . . They've come to give me musical honours . . . I'm a local councillor.'

The little room fills with people. The drums are placed on the chairs, the old banner in a corner, and the spiced wine is passed around. Then, when several bottles have been drunk to the health of Monsieur Frédéric, all fall to discussing gravely the festival: whether the farandole will be as good as last year, whether the bulls will be up to standard; after which the musicians withdraw and go off to give musical honours to the other councillors. At this moment, Mistral's mother arrives.

In no time the table is laid: a beautiful white cloth and two covers. I know the customs of the house; I know that when Mistral has visitors, his mother does not sit at table with them . . . The dear old lady speaks only the Provençal tongue and would not feel at ease talking to Frenchmen . . . Besides, she is needed in the kitchen.

The wonderful meal I had that morning! Slices of roast kid, mountain cheese, must jam, figs, muscatel grapes. All washed down with that excellent châteauneuf des papes which glows in the glasses with such a lovely rose colour . . .

During the dessert, I go and fetch the notebook containing the poem, and lay it on the little table in front of Mistral.

'We said we'd go out,' says the poet, with a smile.
'No, No! ... *Calendal! Calendal!*'
Mistral resigns himself, and in his soft, musical voice, beating the rhythm of his verse with his hand, he begins the first canto:

> Now that I have the sad tale told
> Of a maiden made mad with love,
> I sing, if God wills, of a lad from Cassio,
> A poor little lad, a fisher of anchovy ...

Outside the bells were ringing for Vespers, the fireworks were going off in the square, the fifes and drums were parading up and down the streets. The bulls from the Camargue were bellowing as they were led to the arena.

But I, with my elbows on the tablecloth, and tears in my eyes, I listened to the tale of the little fisher-lad of Provence.

Calendal was not only a fisher-lad; love makes of him a hero ... To win the heart of his beloved – the lovely Estérelle – he undertakes miraculous things, and the twelve labours of Hercules are as nothing beside them.

On one occasion, having made up his mind to become rich, he invented wonderful fishing tackles and brought into harbour all the fish of the sea. Another time, it is the terrible brigand of the Gorge of Ollioules, the Count Sévéran, whom he pursues to his mountain lair itself, amid his cut-throats and his concubines ... A formidable fellow indeed was the young Calendal! One day, on the Sainte-Baume, he encounters two groups of workmen from rival guilds, come there to settle their quarrel by each in turn giving one of the opposing faction an immense buffet on the tomb of Maître Jacques, a Provençal who, if you please, had built the framework for the Temple of Solomon. Calendal hurls himself into the midst of the fray, and pacifies the workmen simply by talking to them ...

Venture follows venture, all of them superhuman! ...
High among the rocks at Lure there was a forest of cedars,
so inaccessible that no woodcutter dared climb there.
Calendal dares. For thirty days he remains alone up there.
For thirty days the sound of his axe is heard cutting deep
into the trunks of the trees. The forest cries out as one after
another of its giants crashes down and falls into the ravines,
and when Calendal comes down again, not one cedar remains
on the mountain ...

At last, in reward for so many great deeds, the fisher-lad
wins the love of Estérelle and is appointed consul by the
people of Cassio. Such is the story of Calendal ... But what
does Calendal matter after all? ... What the poem is about
is Provence – the seas and the mountains of Provence; and
above all, it is about the people of Provence, one people
simple and free, bound together by their history, their
customs, their legends, their landscapes, a people who, in
the hour of their death, have found their great poet ... So
now, build your railways, plant your telegraph poles,
expunge the language of Provence from your school books!
Provence lives forever in *Mireille* and *Calendal*.

'That's enough of poetry!' says Mistral closing his
notebook. 'We must go and see the festival.'

So out we went; the entire village was in the streets; a
strong north wind had swept clean the sky and the sun shone
joyfully on the red roofs, wet with rain. We arrived in time
to see the return of the procession. For an hour we watched
it passing; an endless line of hooded penitents, white
penitents, blue penitents, grey penitents, veiled sisterhoods,
pink banners with golden flowers; big wooden saints,
carried aloft on four shoulders, their gold long since tar-
nished; porcelain saints coloured like idols with huge
bouquets in their hands; copes, monstrances, canopies of
green velvet, crucifixes framed in white silk: it all passed,

the wind blowing it, the candles and the sunshine lighting it, and the psalms, the litanies and the wild pealing of the bells accompanying it.

The procession finished, the saints restored to their chapels, we went to have a look at the bulls, then the games on the village-green, the wrestling, the hop-skip-and-jump, keep-out-the-cat, wine-skin dance, and all the other happy activities of Provençal festivals. Night was falling as we returned to Mistral's house. In the square, in front of the little café where Mistral goes in the evening to have a glass of wine with his friend Zidore, a large bonfire had been lit ... Preparations were being made for the farandole. Lanterns cut out of paper were being lit everywhere in the dark; the young people were preponderant; and soon, at the call of the drums, there began all around the flames a wild romp of a dance that would last the whole night through.

After supper, too tired to go out again, we went up to Mistral's bedroom. It was a modest peasant's room, with two large beds. The walls had no paper on them; on the ceiling the rafters remained exposed ... Four years before, when the Academy awarded a prize of three thousand francs to the author of Mireille, Madame Mistral had had an idea.

'Suppose we paper your bedroom and plaster the ceiling?' she suggested to her son.

'No, no!' replied Mistral. 'That is poet's money. It mustn't be touched.'

And the bedroom stayed quite bare. But, so long as the poet's money lasted, those who knocked on Mistral's door always found his purse open.

I had brought the notebook containing Calendal to the bedroom, and I wanted to get him to read me one more passage before going to sleep. Mistral chose the episode of the porcelain dishes. Here it is in a few words:

The incident occurs during a great feast, held I know not

where. A magnificent service of Moustiers porcelain is placed on the table. Drawn in blue, on the glaze of each plate, is a Provençal subject; the whole history of the land is caught and held in that blue porcelain. And with what love does Mistral describe those beautiful dishes; a stanza to each plate, each one a little poem, the work of simple yet expert craftsmanship, such as was achieved by Theocritus in his little pen-pictures.

While Mistral read me his verses in that beautiful language of Provence which is more than three parts Latin, which queens have spoken, and which only our shepherds now understand, I felt myself overcome with admiration for this man in front of me, and when I thought of the ruined condition in which he had found his mother-tongue and what he has made of it, I imagined to myself one of those old palaces of the princes of Baux that one sees in the Lesser Alps: walls without roofs, stairs without banisters, windows without glass; the trefoils of the Gothic arches broken, the coats of arms above the doorways covered with moss, the courtyards full of scratching hens; pigs wallowing beneath the slender columns of the galleries, donkeys browsing on the grass growing in the chapel, pigeons drinking the rain-water in the great holy-water basins; and lastly, amidst all the decay and the rubbish, a few peasant families who have built themselves huts against the walls of the old palace.

Then, behold, one fine day the son of one of these peasants falls in love with these grand ruins and is filled with indignation at seeing them so profaned; speedily he chases the cattle from the courtyards; and, aided by super-natural powers, all by himself he rebuilds the great stair-case, replaces the wainscoting on the walls and the glass in the windows, raises up the towers, gilds anew the throne room and restores to its former splendour the vast palace of bygone days, where once Popes and Empresses dwelt.

This palace restored is the language of Provence.

Mistral is this peasant's son.

17

The Three Low Masses

A CHRISTMAS TALE

I

'Two truffled turkeys, Garrigou?'

'Yes, your Reverence, two magnificent turkeys stuffed with truffles. I know, because I helped stuff them. The skin had been stretched so tightly you would have thought it was going to burst as it was roasting . . .'

'Jesus-Maria! How I do love truffles! Give me my surplice. Quickly, Garrigou . . . And what else did you see in the kitchen, besides the turkeys? . . .'

'Oh, all sorts of good things . . . Since midday they've done nothing but pluck pheasants, larks, pullets, grouse.

Feathers flying everywhere ... Then they brought eels, carp, trout from the pond and ...

'How big – the trout, Garrigou?'

'As big as that, your Reverence ... Enormous!'

'Merciful heavens! You make me see them ... Have you put the wine in the altar-cruets?'

'Yes, your Reverence, I've put the wine in the altar-cruets ... But you wait and see! It doesn't compare with what you'll be drinking soon, after Midnight Mass. You should see inside the dining-room at the château: decanters blazing bright with wines of all colours ... And the silver dishes, the carved dining-table, the flowers, the candelabra! ... Never will there be a Christmas midnight supper like it. Monsieur le Marquis has invited all the nobility of the neighbourhood. You will be at least forty at table, not counting the bailiff and the scrivener. Ah, you are indeed fortunate to be among them, your Reverence! Just from having sniffed those beautiful turkeys, the smell of the truffles is following me everywhere ... Myum! ...'

'Come now, my son. Let us guard ourselves against the sin of gluttony, especially on the eve of the Nativity ... Off with you, quickly. Light the candles and ring the bell for the first Mass; it is nearly midnight already, and we mustn't be late ...'

This conversation took place one Christmas Eve in the year of grace sixteen hundred and something, between the Reverend Father Balaguère, formerly Prior of the Barnabites, at present Chaplain to the Lords of Trinquelage, and his little clerk Garrigou, for you must know that the devil, on that very evening, had assumed the round face and nondescript features of the young sacristan, the better to lead the reverend father into temptation and make him commit the terrible sin of gluttony. So, whilst the supposed Garrigou (Hem! hm!) was vigorously jingling the bells of the baronial chapel, the reverend father was hastening to

clothe himself in his chasuble in the little sacristy of the
château and, already troubled in spirit by all these gastro-
nomic descriptions, he was repeating to himself as he
dressed,

'Roast turkeys . . . golden carp . . . trout as big as that!...'

Outside, the night wind was blowing, spreading the
music of the bells, and gradually lights were appearing in
the darkness along the slopes of Mont Ventoux, on the top
of which rose the age-old towers of Trinquelage. The
families of the tenant-farmers were coming to hear Midnight Mass at the château. They sang as they climbed the
incline in groups of five or six, the father in front, lantern in
hand, the women swathed in their long, brown cloaks under
which the children huddled for shelter. In spite of the hour
and the cold, all these good folk walked cheerfully, sustained
by the thought that when they came out from Mass there
would be tables laid for them down in the kitchens, as there
were every year. Now and then, on the steep slope, a noble-
man's carriage preceded by torch bearers would twinkle its
windows in the moonlight, or a mule would trot along
tinkling its bells, and by the light of the mist-enveloped
lanterns, the tenants would recognize their bailiff and salute
him as he passed.

'Good evening, good evening, Master Arnoton!'

'Good evening, good evening, friends!'

The night was clear, the stars gleamed bright in the cold
air; the north wind and a fine frozen snow, glancing off the
clothes without wetting them, faithfully maintained the
tradition of a white Christmas. At the very summit of the
slope rose their destination, the château, with its enormous
mass of towers and gables, its chapel spire rising into the
bluish-black sky, and, at all its windows, little lights that
twinkled, bobbing back and forth, and looking, against the
dark background of the building, like sparks flashing in the
ashes of burnt paper . . . Once one was beyond the draw-

bridge and the postern-gate, to reach the chapel it was necessary to cross the outer courtyard, full of carriages, valets and sedan chairs, all brightly lit by the flames of torches and by the blazing kitchen fires. All around could be heard the chinking click of the turnspits, the clatter of pans, the clink of crystal and silver being set out in preparation for a feast; from up above, a warm vapour which smelt of roast meat and potent herbs used for complicated sauces made not only the tenants, but the chaplain, the bailiff, everybody, say:

'What a fine Christmas supper we are going to have after Mass!'

II

Dingdong-dong!... Dingdong-dong!...

So the Midnight Mass begins. In the chapel of the château, a cathedral in miniature, with interlaced arches and oak wainscoting high up the walls, tapestries have been hung, all the candles lit. And the people! The costumes! See first, seated in the carved stalls surrounding the chancel, the Lord of Trinquelage, in salmon-coloured taffeta, and near him all the invited nobility. Opposite, kneeling on prie-Dieus hung with velvet, are the old Dowager Marchioness in her gown of flame-coloured brocade and the young Lady of Trinquelage, wearing on her head the latest fashion of the Court of France: a high tower of fluted lace. Further back, their faces shaved, and wearing black with vast pointed wigs, can be seen the bailiff Thomas Arnoton and the scrivener Master Ambroy, striking two solemn notes among the gaudy silks and brocaded damasks. Then come the fat majordomos, the pages, the grooms, the stewards, the housekeeper with all her keys hung at her side on a fine silver chain. Further back, on benches, are the servants, the maids, and the tenants with their families. And last of all, at the very back, right against the door which they open and shut discreetly, are the scullions who slip in, between sauces, to snatch a little of the atmosphere of the Mass and to bring the smell of the supper into the church, festive and warm with all its lighted candles.

Is it the sight of the scullions' little white caps which distracts the officiating priest? Might it not rather be Garrigou's little bell, that mocking little bell which shakes at the foot of the altar with such infernal haste and seems to keep saying:

'Let's hurry! Let's hurry! The sooner we're finished, the sooner we'll be at supper.'

The fact is that each time this devilish little bell rings, the chaplain forgets his Mass and thinks only of the midnight supper. He imagines the scurrying cooks, the kitchen stoves blazing like blacksmiths' forges, the steam escaping from half-open lids, and, beneath that steam, two magnificent turkeys, stuffed, taut, bursting with truffles . . .

Or still more, he sees pages passing in files carrying dishes surrounded with tempting odours, and he goes with them into the great hall already prepared for the feast. Oh, paradise! He sees the immense table blazing with lights and laden from end to end with peacocks dressed in their feathers, pheasants spreading their wings, flagons the colour of rubies, fruit dazzling bright among green branches, and all the marvellous fish Garrigou was talking about (yes! – Garrigou, of course) displayed on a bed of fennel, their scales pearly as if just from the sea, with bunches of sweet-smelling herbs in their huge nostrils. So real is the vision of these marvels that it seems to Father Balaguère that all these wonderful dishes are served before him on the embroidered altar-cloth, and once – or twice, instead of 'Dominus vobiscum!' he catches himself saying 'Benedicite'. Apart from these slight mistakes, the worthy man recites his office most conscientiously, without missing a line, without omitting one genuflection, and all goes very well until the end of the first Mass; for, as you know, the same priests must celebrate three consecutive Masses on Christmas Day.

'One over!' says the chaplain to himself with a sigh of relief; then, without wasting a moment, he signs to his clerk, or him whom he thinks is his clerk, and—

Dingdong-dong! . . . Dingdong-dong! . . .

So the second Mass begins, and with it begins also the sin of Father Balaguère.

'Quick, quick, let's hurry!' Garrigou's little bell cries to him in its shrill little voice, and this time the unfortunate priest abandons himself completely to the demon of gluttony, hurls himself on the missal and devours the pages with the avidity of his over-stimulated appetite. Frantically he kneels, rises, makes vague signs of the cross, half-genuflects, cuts short all his gestures in order to finish the sooner. He scarcely extends his arms at the Gospel, or beats his breast at the *Confiteor*. It is between the clerk and himself who will jabber the quicker. Verses and responses patter pell-mell, buffeting each other. Words half-pronounced without opening the mouth which would take too much time, die away in a baffling hum.

'*Oremus ps . . . ps . . . ps . . .*'
'*Mea culpa . . . pa . . . pa . . .*'

Like hurrying wine-harvesters treading the grapes, both splatter about in the latin of the Mass, sending splashes in all directions.

'*Dom . . . scum ! . . .*,' says Balaguère.

'. . . *Stutuo . . .*,' replies Garrigou; and all the time that damned little bell is ringing in their ears, like those bells they put on post-horses to make them gallop quicker. Obviously at this pace a Low Mass is quickly got out of the way.

'Two over!' says the chaplain quite out of breath; then, red and sweating, without pausing to recover, he rushes down the altar steps and . . .

Ding-dong!... Dingdong-dong!...

So the third Mass begins. It is not far now to the dining hall; but, alas, the nearer the midnight supper approaches, the more the unfortunate Balaguère feels himself seized by a gluttonous madness of impatience. He even sees more distinctly the golden carp, the roast turkeys ... There!... Yes, and there!... He touches them ... he ... Oh, merciful heavens! ... the dishes are steaming, the wines are ambrosial, and, shaking itself madly, the little bell is shrieking at him:

'Quick, quick! Be more quick!'

But how could he go more quickly? His lips are scarcely moving. He is no longer pronouncing the words ... Unless he cheats the good God completely and omits part of the Mass ... And that is exactly what the wretched man does! Falling deeper into temptation, he begins by skipping one verse, then two. Then the Epistle is too long so he doesn't finish it; he skims through the Gospel, passes over the Creed, jumps the Pater, bows distantly to the Preface, and thus by leaps and bounds hurls himself into eternal damnation, closely followed by the infamous Garrigou (*vade, retro, Satanus!*) who cooperates splendidly, holding up his chasuble, turning the pages two at a time, knocking over the desks, upsetting the altar-cruets, and ceaselessly shaking that tiny little bell, louder and louder, quicker and quicker.

The startled faces of the congregation are a sight to behold! Obliged to join in a Mass conducted in dumb-show by a priest whose words they can't hear, some stand up as others are kneeling, or sit when others are rising. And every succeeding part of this extraordinary service results in a confused variety of postures on all the benches. The Star of the Nativity, journeying up there across the sky towards the little stable, paled with apprehension at the sight of such disorder.

'The priest is going too quickly ... you can't keep up

with him,' the old Dowager grumbles, shaking her coif angrily.

Master Arnoton, his large steel spectacles on his nose, searches in his prayer-book, wondering where the deuce they are up to. But, on the whole, all these worthy folk are themselves also thinking of the supper, and are not sorry the Mass is going at top speed. And when Father Balaguère, his face shining radiantly, turns towards the congregation and shouts at the top of his voice: '*Ite, missa est,*' the whole chapel replies, as one voice, with a '*Deo Gratias*' so merry and so lively you would have thought they were already at table responding to the first toast.

III

Five minutes later, all the nobles were taking their seats in the great hall, the chaplain in the midst of them. The château, bright with lights in every room, was reverberating with songs, shouts, laughter, uproar everywhere; and the venerable Father Balaguère was plunging his fork into the wing of the grouse, drowning remorse for his sin under floods of wine and rich meat gravy. The unfortunate holy man drank so much and ate so much, he died of a stroke that night without even having time to repent. In the morning, he arrived in heaven still all in a stupor after the night's feasting and I leave you to ponder over the reception he was given.

'Get out of My sight, you wicked Christian!' the Sovereign Judge, Master of us all, said to him, 'Your lapse from virtue is so great it outweighs all the goodness of your life. You stole from Me a Midnight Mass. Well, you will pay it back three-hundred-fold. You will not enter Paradise until you have celebrated three hundred Christmas Masses in your own chapel and in the presence of all those who sinned with you and by your fault.'

. ... Such, in truth, is the legend of Father Balaguère, as you will hear it told in the land of olives. Today the Château de Trinquelage no longer exists, but the chapel still stands on the summit of Mont Ventoux, in a clump of holly oaks. Its disjointed door bangs in the wind, its threshold is overgrown with weeds; there are nests in the corners of the altar and in the recesses of the huge casement windows from which the coloured glass has long since disappeared. Yet it is said that at Christmas every year a supernatural light hovers among these ruins, and that peasants, going to Mass and the midnight supper in the church since built below, see this ghost of a chapel lit with invisible candles which burn in the open air even in wind and snow. You may laugh if you will, but a local vine-grower named Garrigue, a descendant no doubt of Garrigou, has assured me that one Christmas Eve, being slightly drunk, he had lost his way on the mountain near Trinquelage; and this is what he saw . . . Until eleven o'clock, nothing. Suddenly, towards midnight, a peal of bells sounded high in the steeple, an old peal not heard for many many years and seeming to come from many leagues away. Soon after, on the path leading upwards, Garrigue saw lights flickering, faint shadows moving. Under the chapel porch there were footsteps, voices whispering:

'Good evening, Master Arnoton!'

'Good evening, good evening, friends!'

When everyone had entered, my vine-grower, who was very brave, approached softly, looked through the broken door, and saw a strange sight. All these people he had seen passing were ranged in rows around the chancel, in the ruined nave, as if the ancient benches were still there. Beautiful ladies in brocade with coifs of lace, handsome noblemen bedecked from head to foot, peasants in flowered jackets such as our grandfathers wore; everything appeared faded, dusty, old and tired. From time to time night birds, the residents now of the chapel, woken by all the lights, came swooping around the candles whose flames burned erect yet nebulous, as if hidden behind a thin veil. And what amused Garrigue greatly was a certain person wearing large steel spectacles who kept shaking his tall black wig on which one of these birds stood, entangled, silently flapping its wings . . .

At the far end, a little old man no taller than a child was kneeling in the centre of the chancel, shaking despairingly a little, tongueless, soundless bell; while a priest clothed in old gold moved back and fro before the altar reciting prayers no word of which could be heard . . . It was, most surely, Father Balaguère saying his third Low Mass.

18

The Oranges

SOME VISUAL MEMORIES

IN Paris, oranges have a sad look, as of windfalls picked up
from under a tree. In the middle of cold, wet winters, the
time of year they reach you, their brilliantly coloured peel,
their scent – which seems exaggerated in countries accustomed to milder flavours – gives them a foreign air, slightly
bohemian. On misty evenings, piled in their little hand-
barrows, under the dim light of a red paper lantern, they
pass sadly along the edge of the pavements. A thin monotonous cry, lost in the noise and clatter of carriage wheels
and omnibuses, accompanies them:

'A penny each! Valencia oranges!'

Three quarters of Parisians regard this fruit from so far
away, with its round shape so unremarkable and with only a
bit of green from its tree remaining attached to it, as a sort
of sweetmeat or confectionery. The tissue paper around it,
the festive occasions on which it is eaten, contribute to this
impression. Especially around the beginning of January, the
thousands of oranges scattered about the streets, the peel
lying in the mud of the gutters, make you think of some
gigantic Christmas tree shaking its branches laden with
artificial fruit over Paris. Not a corner where you do not see
them. In lighted shop windows carefully selected and
arranged; outside the gates of prisons and hospitals among
the packets of biscuits and the piles of apples, at the
entrances to dance-halls and Sunday shows. And their
exquisite smell is mixed with the odour of gas, the noise of

fiddles and the dust of the theatre galleries. All this tends to make us forget that oranges come from orange trees, for the fruit comes to us direct from the south in bulging packing cases, while the tree makes only a brief appearance in our public gardens when it is brought forth, clipped, transformed and disguised, into the open air from the hot-house where it has spent the winter.

Really to know oranges, you must see them where they belong, in the Balearic Islands, in Sardinia, in Corsica, in Algeria, in the golden-blue air, the warm atmosphere of the Mediterranean. I recall a little orange grove outside the gates of Blidah; that is where they are beautiful! Amidst the dark, lustrous, varnished foliage the fruit had the vivid brilliance of stained glass and made the surrounding air golden with that halo of splendour which surrounds vividly brilliant flowers. Here and there, gaps between the branches allowed a view of the ramparts of the little town, the minaret of the mosque, the dome of a shrine and, over all, the enormous mass of the Atlas Mountains, green at their base, crowned with snow like a mantle of white fur frizzed in places the wrong way – the patches of newly fallen snow.

One night, during my stay there, owing to some inexplicable phenomenon unknown for thirty years, this belt of frosty winter shook itself over the sleeping town, and Blidah awoke transformed, powdery-white. In this so pure, so rare air of Algeria, the snow seemed like dust of mother-of-pearl. It had the sheen of white peacock feathers.

Most beautiful was the orange grove. The solid leaves kept the snow compact and intact like ice-cream on lacquered plates and each orange with its powdering of frosty snow had a splendid smoothness, an unobtrusive radiance, like gold beneath a veil of white gossamer. It gave, somehow, an impression of church festivals, of red soutanes under lace robes, of altar gildings covered with guipures . . .

But my most cherished memory of oranges comes to me from Barbicaglia, a large garden near Ajaccio where I used to go for my siesta in the heat of the day. Here the orange trees, taller and more widely spaced than at Blidah, descended as far as the road which was separated from the garden by only a hedge and a ditch. Immediately beyond was the sea, the immense, blue sea . . . What happy hours I passed in this garden! Over my head, the orange trees, in full bloom of flower and fruit, distilled in the burning heat the sheer essence of their scent. From time to time, a ripe orange, as if heavy with heat, would suddenly detach itself and fall near me on the open ground with a dull, echoless thud. I had only to stretch out my hand. Purple-red inside, they were superb fruit. They seemed to me exquisite; and then so beautiful was the horizon! The sea interwove dazzling blue spaces between the leaves, like pieces of broken glass glittering in the hazy air. And filling the air all around was the movement of the waves, their murmuring rhythm lulling you like the rise and fall of an invisible boat. And the heat . . . And the scent of the oranges . . . Oh, yes, how good, how very good it was to sleep in Barbicaglia garden!

Sometimes, however, at the best moment of my siesta, the rat-a-tat of drums used to wake me with a start. It was those wretched amateur drummers come to practise down below on the road. Through the holes in the hedge I would see the brass of the drums and the big white aprons over their red trousers. To protect themselves from the blinding light piti-lessly reflected by the white dust of the road, the poor devils used to come and stand at the foot of the garden, in the narrow shade from the hedge. And they beat their drums! And they were hot! Then, shaking myself forcibly out of my hypnotic slumber, I used to amuse myself by throwing at them a few of the lovely golden-red oranges hanging near my hand. The drummer aimed at would stop. There would be a moment's hesitation, a look around to see where the superb orange rolling in the ditch in front of him came from; then he would snatch it up and take an enormous bite without even peeling it.

I remember, too, that right next to Barbicaglia, and separated from it only by a little low wall, was a rather bizarre little garden which I could see into from my higher position. It was a small patch of ground, laid out quite ordinarily. Its sandy yellow paths bordered with deep-green box-trees, the two cypresses at its gateway, gave it the look of one of the country house gardens around Marseilles. At the far end, a white stone building had ventilation openings at ground level as for a wine cellar. At first I had thought it was a country house; but on closer examination, I realized from the cross on its roof, from an inscription carved in the stone which I could make out without being able to read, that it was a Corsican family tomb. All around Ajaccio, there are many of these mortuary chapels standing in the midst of gardens entirely on their own. There the family comes each Sunday, to visit its dead. Seen in this way, death is less terrible than in the crowded confusion of cemeteries. Only the step of friends disturbs the silence.

From where I was, I used to see a kindly-looking old man trotting sedately along the paths. All day long he pruned the trees, dug, watered, removed the wilted flowers with minute care; then, at the setting of the sun, he would enter the little chapel where his family's dead were sleeping; he would replace the spade, the rake, the large watering cans; all was done tranquilly, with the serenity of a graveyard gardener. Yet, without his at all being aware of it, this good man worked with a kind of reverence, softening all noises and gently closing the door of the vault each time, as if he feared to waken someone. In the great, radiant silence, his care for that little garden disturbed not one bird, and it had nothing of sadness about it. It only made the sea seem more immense, the sky more high; and this siesta without end, amid the ever-restless, ever-triumphant life-forces of nature, diffused all around it the feeling of eternal rest.

19

The Two Inns

IT was while returning from Nîmes, one July afternoon. The weather was oppressively hot. As far as eye could see, clouds of dust hung over the burning white road between the gardens of olive trees and a few dwarf oak trees, under a huge sun of dullish silver which filled the whole sky. Not a patch of shade, not a breath of wind. Nothing but the quivering of the hot air and the strident cry of the cicadas, that crazy, deafening, urgent music whose loudness seemed the equivalent in sound of this immense quivering radiance ... I had been walking for two hours without seeing a soul, when suddenly a cluster of white houses rose up in front of me through the dust of the road. They were what is called the posting station of Saint-Vincent: five or six small farmhouses, a few long, red-roofed barns, a drinking trough without water under a clump of lean fig-trees, and beyond them all, two large inns facing each other on either side of the road.

The proximity of these inns was somehow startling. On one side, a large new building, full of life and movement, all its doors open, the coach drawn up in front, the steaming horses being unharnessed, the passengers having a quick drink on the roadside in the narrow shade of the walls; its yard a jumble of mules and carts; carriers lying under the sheds, waiting the cool of the evening. Inside, shouts, curses, banging of fists on tables, clatter of glasses, click of billiards, popping of lemonade corks, and, over-riding all this uproar, a voice singing, loudly, joyously, making all the windows shake:

Margoton the lovely,
Each morn rose up early,
Her silver pitcher to fill
With water from the well . . .

. . . The inn opposite was, in contrast, silent and apparently deserted. Grass in the gateway, shutters broken, on the door a mildewed holly bough hanging like a reminder of glory departed, the door steps wedged with stones from the road . . . Everything so poor, so pitiful, that it truly would be an act of charity to stop and have a drink there.

On entering, I found a long, drab, empty room which the dazzling light through the three large uncurtained windows made still more empty and drab. Even the furniture seemed asleep: some rickety tables on which stood a few dusty glasses, a billiard table holding out its torn pockets as if they were beggar's bowls, a yellow sofa, an old counter. And flies! Flies! I have never seen so many; on the ceiling, sticking to the window panes, on the glasses, whole clusters of them . . . When I opened the door, it caused a buzzing, a whirling of wings as if I had entered a hive.

At the back of the room, in the recess of a casement window there was a woman standing, completely absorbed in what she was looking at outside. I called to her twice:

'Hey, there! Mistress!'

She turned slowly, so that I was able to take in her poor peasant woman's face, lined, wrinkled, the colour of earth, encircled by long pinners of reddish-brown lace such as our old women wear. Yet this was not an old woman; rather she was one who had known sorrow too soon and too deeply.

'What is it you want?' she asked, wiping her eyes.

'To sit a moment and drink something.'

She gave me a look full of astonishment, without moving from the window, as if she did not understand.

'This isn't an inn, then?'

The woman sighed.

'Yes ... you can call it an inn, if you like ... But why don't you go over there like the others? It's much more lively ...'

'Too lively for me ... I'd rather stay here.'

And without waiting for an answer, I seated myself at a table.

When she was quite sure I was speaking seriously, she began to move about with a very busy air, opening drawers, moving bottles, wiping glasses, disturbing the flies ... It made one feel that a customer was quite an event. Now and then the poor woman stopped and held her head as if she despaired of doing what she had to do.

Then she went off into the room at the back. I heard her rattling large keys, struggling with locks, rummaging in the bread bin, blowing, dusting, washing plates. From time to time there came a long-drawn-out sigh, a half-smothered sob ...

After a quarter of an hour of these goings on, I had before me a plate of raisins, an old Beaucaire loaf as hard as grit, and a bottle of inferior local wine.

'You are served,' said the strange creature, and returned quickly to her place at the window.

While I drank, I tried to make her talk.

'You don't often have people here, do you?'

'No, monsieur, never a soul! When we were on our own here it was different: then we had the posting station, meals during the duck-shooting season, carriages stopping all the year round ... But since the people over the way came, we've lost everything ... Everybody prefers to go there. It's too dull for them here ... It's no use pretending it isn't. I've lost all my looks, I keep having feverish attacks since my two little girls died ... Over there it's just the opposite. Everybody always laughing and joking. A woman from

Arles runs it. A real beauty, with lace and gold round her neck. The coach driver's her lover, so he stops the coach there now. And all the chamber maids are the coaxing, come-hither sort. That helps to bring the money in as well! She gets all the young fellows from Bezonces, Redessan, and Jonquières. The carriers go out of their way just to call now she's there . . . And I, I'm stuck here all day without a soul, breaking my heart.'

She said all this in an apathetic voice, her forehead still

pressed against the window pane. Obviously there was something about the inn opposite preying very much on her mind.

All at once, on the other side of the road, there was a great commotion. The coach was moving off in a cloud of dust. Whips could be heard cracking, a fanfare of the postilion's horn, girls shouting as they ran to the door: Good-bye! ... Good-bye! ... and above it all that same tremendous voice ringing out more beautifully than before:

> Her silver pitcher to fill
> With water from the well;
> She saw not on the hill
> Three knights all arm'd full well ...

At the sound of this voice my hostess shivered from head to foot and, turning to me, said in a low voice:

'D'you hear? That's my husband ... He does sing well, doesn't he?'

I looked at her dumbfounded.

'What? Your husband! ... He goes over there also?'

Then, heartbrokenly, but with a great gentleness:

'What can you expect, monsieur? That is how men are. They don't like tears. And I am always weeping since my little ones died. And it's so sad, this big house, where there's never a soul ... So when he gets too bored, my poor José goes and has a drink over there, and he's such a wonderful voice the woman from Arles makes him sing. Listen! ... There ... he's beginning again.'

And, trembling, with her hands raised and with huge tears making her still uglier, she stood there at the window as if in an ecstatic trance, listening to her José singing for the woman from Arles:

> First of all he said to her:
> 'Good day, my pretty one,
>   My sweet one.'

20

At Milianah

NOTES MADE DURING A JOURNEY

THIS time I am taking you to spend the day in a small, pleasant Algerian town some few hundred leagues from Paris. It will be a little change from drums and cicadas . . .

. . . It is going to rain, the sky is grey, mist shrouds the peaks of Mount Zaccar. A miserable Sunday . . . I am trying to pass the time smoking cigarettes in my little hotel bedroom through whose open window I can see the ramparts of this little Arab town. I have had all the hotel library put at my disposal; in between a detailed history of wills and probate and some novels by Paul de Kock, I discover an odd volume of Montaigne. Opening the book at random, I reread the admirable letter on the death of Boethius . . . With the result that I am more gloomy and depressed than ever. A few drops of rain are falling already. As they land on the window ledge, each drop forms a large star in the dust heaped up there since last year's rains . . . The book slips out of my hand and for a long while I gaze at those melancholy stars.

Two o'clock strikes from the town clock – on the side of an ancient shrine whose slender white walls are all I can see from here . . . Poor old shrine, it could never have thought, thirty years ago, that one day it would have a huge municipal dial stuck in the middle of its chest, and that at two o'clock every Sunday it would give the signal to all the churches of Milianah to ring for vespers! . . . Ding! Dong! Now all the bells are at it! . . . They'll go on like that for quite a while

... Most definitely, this room is depressing. The immense spiders that come out in the morning, those they call philosophical thoughts, have spun their webs in every corner ... Let's go out.

I reach the main square. Not put off by a little rain, the band of the 3rd regiment of the line has just grouped itself around its conductor. At one of the barrack's windows, the General appears, surrounded by his daughters; in the square the Sub-Prefect is walking up and down arm-in-arm with the Justice of the Peace. Half a dozen half-naked little Arab boys, shouting fiercely, are playing marbles in a corner. Down below, an old Jew in rags comes searching for the sunshine he had left at that spot yesterday and is astonished not to find it there any more. 'One, two, three, off!' The band strikes up an old mazurka by Talexy, which the barrel organs used to play under my windows last winter. This mazurka used to annoy me then; today it moves me to tears.

Ah, happy bandsmen of the 3rd! Eyes fixed on the double crotchets, drunk with rhythm and noise, they think of nothing but keeping time. Their soul, their whole being is bound up in that piece of paper no wider than their hand – which quivers at the end of their instrument between two brass teeth. 'One, two, three, off!' That's all that matters to these good people; the national airs they play have never made them homesick ... Alas! I am not part of their band; this music hurts me, and I go away ...

Where could I go to pass this dismal Sunday afternoon? Of course! Sid' Omar's shop is open ... We'll call on Sid' Omar.

Although he has a shop, Sid' Omar is not a shop-keeper. He is a prince of the blood, the son of a former Dey of Algiers who died strangled by the janissaries ... At the death of his father, Sid' Omar took refuge in Milianah with his mother whom he adored, and lived there for some years, a great lord and philosopher, with his greyhounds, his hawks, his horses and his wives, in cool, charming palaces abounding with fountains and orange trees. Then came the French. Sid' Omar, at first our enemy and the ally of Abd-el-Kader, ended by quarrelling with the Emir and made his submission. To avenge himself, the Emir entered Milianah while Sid' Omar was away, plundered his palaces, destroyed his orange groves, took away his horses and his wives, and had his mother's throat crushed beneath the lid of a huge chest ... Sid' Omar's anger was terrible: immediately he entered the service of France and we had no better nor fiercer soldier than he while the war against the Emir lasted. The war over, Sid' Omar came back to Milianah; but even today, if one mentions the name of Abd-el-Kader, he goes pale and his eyes glitter.

Sid' Omar is sixty. Despite his age and smallpox, his face is still handsome; long eyelashes, the glance of a woman, a charming smile, the air of a prince. Ruined by the war, he retains of his former wealth only a farm on the Chélif plain and a house in Milianah where he lives carefully with the three sons he has brought up himself. The native chieftains hold him in great veneration. When an argument arises, he is willingly accepted as arbitrator, and his judgement is nearly always accepted as law. He seldom goes out, and is to be found every afternoon in a shop which adjoins his house and which opens on to the street. The furniture there is not expensive: white-washed walls, a circular bench, some cushions, some long pipes, two braziers ... It is there that Sid' Omar gives audiences and dispenses justice. A Solomon enthroned in a shop.

As today is Sunday, there is a large attendance. All around the room a dozen chieftains in their white robes are seated on the floor with their knees crossed. Each has a large pipe and a little cup of coffee in a filigree holder beside him. I enter, nobody moves ... From his seat, Sid' Omar greets my entrance with his most charming smile and invites me with a wave of his hand to seat myself near him on a large cushion of yellow silk; then, a finger to his lips, he signs to me to listen.

This is the case: The Caid of the Beni-Zougzougs has had some disagreement with a Jew of Milianah about a plot of ground and the two parties have agreed to bring the matter before Sid' Omar and to accept his decision. An appointment has been made for that very day, the witnesses are summoned; suddenly behold the Jew changes his mind and comes alone, without witnesses, to declare that he would rather leave it to the French Justice of the Peace than to Sid' Omar ... That is where the matter stands on my arrival.

The Jew – old, bearded and cadaverous, with maroon coat and velvet cap – raises his face to heaven, rolls imploring eyes, kisses Sid' Omar's slipper, bows his head, kneels, clasps his hands. I do not understand Arabic, but from the Jew's pantomime, from the words *Justice of the Peace*, *Justice of the Peace*, which recur every moment, I can guess the whole of his fine speech:

'We do not doubt Sid' Omar, Sid' Omar is wise, Sid' Omar is just ... All the same, the *Justice of the Peace* will arrange our little affair better.'

The audience is indignant, but being Arab remains impassive ... Reclining on his cushion, his eyes expressionless, the amber mouthpiece of his pipe between his lips, Sid' Omar – an ironical god – smiles as he listens. Suddenly, at the height of his eloquence, the Jew is interrupted by a full-throated *¡Caramba!* which stops him short. At the same moment, a Spanish colonist, present as a witness for the Caid, leaves his place, goes up to the Jew, and hurls at him a flood of colourful and multi-lingual abuse, including a certain French word too coarse to be repeated here ... Sid' Omar's son, understanding French, blushes at hearing such a word in his father's presence and goes out of the room. Note this characteristic of Arab breeding. The audience remains impassive; Sid' Omar is still smiling. The Jew has got up and is retreating backwards to the door, trembling with fear, but babbling still louder his ceaseless *Justice of the Peace, Justice of the Peace* ... He goes out. The Spaniard, furious, hurls himself after him, catches him in the street and – bing! bang! – hits him full in the face twice ... The Jew falls to his knees, his arms outstretched ... The Spaniard, a little ashamed, comes back into the shop. As soon as he has gone, the Jew gets up and gives a crafty look at the motley crowd all around him. People of every colour are there – Maltese, Mahonese, negroes, Arabs – all united in their hatred of Jews and delighted at seeing one of them treated roughly. Our Jew hesitates a moment, then, catching an Arab by the hem of his robe,

'You saw him, Achmed, you saw him ... You were there ... The Christian hit me ... You will bear witness ... that is good ... You will bear witness.'

The Arab releases his robe and pushes the Jew away. He knows nothing, he saw nothing: at that very moment he had been looking the other way.

'But you, Kaddour, you saw him ... you saw the Christian beat me ...' cries the unfortunate Jew to a fat negro busy peeling a prickly pear.

The negro spits to show his contempt and goes off; he has seen nothing. Nor has that little Maltese, his eyes gleaming spitefully beneath his cap. Nor that brick-coloured Mahonese woman, who laughs as she turns away with her basket of pomegranates on her head ...

The Jew has shouted, prayed, scurried here and there ... not one witness! Nobody saw anything ... As luck would have it, two of his co-religionists come slinking along the street at that moment, keeping close to the wall. The Jew spots them:

'Quick, quick, brothers! Make haste to the lawyer! Make haste to the Justice of the Peace! You saw him, both of you . . . You saw him beat an old man!'

Had they seen him! . . . I should say they had!

. . . Great excitement in Sid' Omar's shop . . . The owner of the café refills the cups, relights the pipes. Everybody is chattering and laughing loudly. It's so amusing seeing a Jew beaten up! . . . In the midst of the hubbub and smoke, I make quietly for the door; I have a wish to go and prowl a little in the Jewish quarter to find out how the Jew's co-religionists have taken the insult to their brother.

'Come and dine this evening, *moussiou*,' the kind-hearted Sid' Omar calls after me . . .

I accept, I thank him. Then I am outside.

In the Jewish quarter everybody is afoot. The affair is already on everybody's lips. Nobody in the shops. Embroiderers, tailors, saddlers – all Israel is on the streets. The men – wearing velvet caps and blue woollen stockings – are gesticulating noisily in groups . . . The women, pale, puffy, stiff as wooden idols in their dull gowns with golden bodice-fronts, their faces encircled with narrow black bands, go caterwauling from one group to the next. Just as I arrive, there is a surging movement in the crowd. Everybody rushes and presses forward . . . Leaning on his witnesses, the Jew – hero of the hour – passes between two rows of caps to a shower of exhortations:

'Avenge yourself, brother; avenge yourself, avenge the Jewish people. Fear nothing; the law is with you.'

A horrible dwarf, smelling of old leather and cobbler's wax, comes up to me looking woeful and sighing deeply.

'You see,' he says. 'How they treat us poor Jews! An old man as well. Look! They nearly killed him.'

In truth, the poor Jew looks more dead than alive. He passes in front of me – his eyes are lifeless, his face haggard, not walking, being dragged along ... Only heavy damages can cure him; that is why they are not taking him to the doctor, but to the lawyer.

Lawyers are numerous in Algeria – almost as many as locusts. It seems business is good. In any case, it has the advantage that you can practise without any difficulty – no examinations, no sureties, no indentures. Just as we become writers in Paris, so they become lawyers in Algeria. The only requirements are to know a bit of French, Spanish, Arabic, to have a legal code always up your sleeve, and above all to have the right temperament.

The lawyer's functions are very varied: in turn advocate, attorney, broker, valuer, interpreter, book-keeper, commission-agent, public-scribe, he is the Maître Jacques of the colony. Harpagon, however, had only one Maître Jacques, and the colony has more than it needs. At Milianah alone there are dozens of them. Usually, to avoid the expense of an office, these gentlemen receive their clients in the café in the main square and give advice – give it? – between an absinthe and a coffee with rum.

It is towards the café in the main square that the worthy Jew is making his way, flanked by his two witnesses. We'll not follow them.

On leaving the Jewish quarter, I pass the Arab Bureau. From outside, with its slate roof and the French flag flying above it, you would take it for the *mairie* of a French village. I know the interpreter, so let's go in and smoke a cigarette with him. From one cigarette to the next I'll manage to survive this sun-less Sunday!

The courtyard of the Bureau is cluttered with Arabs in ragged clothes. There are about fifty of them, squatting along the wall in their burnous, awaiting an interview.

Although it's in the open air, this Bedouin antechamber smells strongly of human skins. Let's pass quickly ... In the Bureau, I find the interpreter having difficulties with two big vociferous fellows entirely naked under their long dirty blankets. They are relating with excited mimicry some tale about a stolen rosary. I sit down on a straw mat in a corner and watch ... A handsome uniform these interpreters have; and it certainly suits the Milianah interpreter! He and the uniform look as if they've been made for each other. It is sky-blue with black loops and shining gold buttons. The interpreter is fair, fresh-complexioned, with curly hair; a handsome blue hussar full of freakish humour; a little talkative – he speaks so many languages – a little sceptical – he knew Renan at the School of Oriental Languages! – a great lover of sport, at his ease in the Sub-Prefect's wife's drawing-room. In short, a Parisian. That is our man and you must not be surprised that the ladies are mad about him. As a dandy, he has only one rival, the sergeant of the Arab Bureau, with his tunic of fine cloth and his gaiters with mother-of-pearl buttons, that fellow is the envy and despair of the whole garrison. Seconded to the Arab Bureau, he is excused all fatigues and is always to be seen about the streets, white-gloved, freshly-curled, with large registers under his arm. He is admired and feared. He is one with authority.

This tale about the stolen rosary definitely threatens to be exceedingly long. Good evening! I'll not wait for the end.

I find the antechamber in an uproar as I go out. The crowd is surging round a tall Algerian, pale, proud, draped in a black burnous. A week ago this man had a fight with a panther on the Zaccar. The panther died; but the man had half his arm eaten. Every morning and evening he comes to have his wounds dressed at the Arab Bureau, and each time they stop him to make him tell his story. He speaks slowly in a beautiful throaty voice. From time to time he draws aside his burnous and shows his left arm bound to his chest and swathed in bloodstained bandages.

I am scarcely in the street when a violent storm breaks. Rain, thunder, lightning, sirocco . . . Quick, let's shelter. I slip through the first door and find myself in the midst of a band of gipsies crowded together under the arches of a Moorish courtyard. This courtyard belongs to the mosque of Milianah; it's the customary refuge for Mohammedan poverty. They call it 'The Court of the Poor'.

Big skinny greyhounds, all covered with vermin, come prowling round me threateningly. With my back against one of the pillars of the gallery I try to look unconcerned, and, without speaking to anyone, I watch the rain bouncing off the coloured paving-stones of the courtyard. The gipsies are heaped together on the ground. Near me, her throat and legs bare, with big iron bracelets on her wrists and ankles, a young, almost beautiful woman is singing a strange melody on three notes, nasal and melancholy. As she sings she feeds at her breast a little child, quite naked and the colour of red bronze. With her free arm, she grinds barley in a stone mortar. The rain, driven by a cruel wind, occasionally soaks her legs and the body of the child she nurses. The gipsy woman takes not the slightest heed and as the storm continues she sings on, crushing the barley and feeding her child.

The storm is dying down. Taking advantage of a lull in the wind, I hasten to leave the Court of Miracles and I make for Sid' Omar's; it is time for his dinner . . . While crossing the square, I again come across my old friend the Jew. He is leaning on his lawyer; his witnesses walk happily behind him. They are all radiant with joy. The lawyer has accepted his case: he will ask the court for two thousand francs damages.

*

A magnificent dinner at Sid' Omar's. – The dining-room opens on to an elegant Moorish courtyard full of the music of the fountains ... I recommend the excellent Turkish meal to Baron Brisse. Among other dishes I note especially *poulet aux amandes*, *couscous à la vanille*, *tortue à la viande* – a little heavy but deliciously seasoned – and honey biscuits called *bouchées de Kadi* ... For wine, nothing but champagne. In spite of Moslem law, Sid' Omar drinks a little – when the servants' backs are turned ... After dinner, we adjourn to our host's bedroom where we are served with sweetmeats, pipes and coffee. The furnishings of this room are of the simplest – a divan, a few rush mats; at the far end a large, very high bed on which little red, gold-embroidered cushions are scattered ... On the wall hangs an old Turkish painting portraying the exploits of a certain Admiral Hamadi. Artists in Turkey, it seems, use only one colour for each painting: this one is devoted to green. The sea, sky, ships, Admiral Hamadi himself, are all green, and what a green! ...

Arab custom requires one to leave early. Coffee drunk, pipes smoked, I bid good night to my host and leave him to the company of his wives.

Where shall I end my evening? It is too early for bed. Besides, I wouldn't be able to sleep; Sid' Omar's gold cushions are dancing fantastic farandoles all round me ... Here is the theatre; let's go in for a moment.

The theatre of Milianah is an old fodder warehouse, more or less disguised as a place of entertainment. Huge lamps, refilled with oil during the interval, supply the lighting. In the pit one has to stand; in the orchestra stalls are benches. The galleries are very select: they have straw-bottomed chairs. All round the auditorium, a long, dark, unpaved corridor ... You would think you were out in the street, nothing is different ... The play has already started when I arrive. To my great surprise, the actors are not bad: the men, that is; they have zest, life . . . Being mostly amateurs, soldiers of the 3rd, the regiment is proud of them and comes every evening to applaud.

As for the women, alas . . . Here as everywhere they are the eternal females of little provincial theatres, pretentious, exaggerated, false. Amongst them, however, are two who interest me – two Milianah Jewesses, quite young, making their stage debut. Their parents are in the audience and appear enchanted. They are convinced their daughters are going to make millions in this business. The legend of Rachel, Jewess, millionairess and actress, has already spread to the Jews of the Orient.

Nothing could be more comical and yet more moving than those two little Jewesses on the stage. They keep themselves timidly to one corner of the set – powder over their make-up, rigid in their low-necked costumes. They are cold, they are ashamed. Now and then they jabber a sentence uncomprehendingly, and, as they do so, their large Hebrew eyes gaze in amazement out into the auditorium.

I leave the theatre . . . In the darkness surrounding me, I hear shouts coming from a corner of the square . . . Some Maltese, probably having it out with knives.

I return slowly along the ramparts to the hotel. Delicious scents of orange trees and thuyas mount from the plain. The air is soft, the sky almost clear . . . Down there, at the end of that path, stands an old ghost of a wall, fragment of some ancient temple. It is holy, this wall: every day Arab women come and hang votive offerings on it, bits of clothing, long tresses of red hair bound with silver thread, skirts of burnous . . . All are there, fluttering in the pale moonlight, wafted by the warm, night air.

21

The Locusts

ONE more memory of Algeria, and then we shall return to the mill . . .

The night I arrived at the farm at Sahel I could not sleep. The new country, the excitement of the journey, the barking of the jackals, then an enervating oppressive heat, a complete suffocation, as if not a breath of air could pass through the meshes of the mosquito netting . . . When I opened my window at dawn, a heavy summer mist, its edges tinged with black and rose, was swirling slowly, drifting like a cloud of cannon powder on a battlefield. Not a leaf was moving and everything in the beautiful garden before me – the vines spaced out on the slope to catch the burning sun which makes sweet wine, the fruit trees from Europe sheltered in a shady corner, the little orange trees, the tangerine trees in their long minuscule rows – all had the same mournful look, the immobility of leaves awaiting a storm. Even the banana trees, those tall, tender, green reeds, whose delicate fine tresses are always agitated by the slightest breath of air, stood silent and erect, orderly files of plumes.

I remained for a moment gazing at this wonderful plantation where all the trees of the world were gathered together, each giving its flower and fruit at the season appropriate to its country of origin. Between the fields of wheat and the clumps of cork-oaks, a water-course sparkled, a refreshing sight on this stifling morning; and as I stood admiring the orderly luxuriance of these things, of the beautiful farmhouse with its Moorish arcades, its terraces so white in the dawn, of the stables and outhouses surrounding it, I thought of the time these good people came to settle in this valley of Sahel twenty years before, and of how they found only a ramshackle, road-mender's hut and an uncultivated land overgrown with dwarf palms and lentisks. Everything had to be built, created, in the face of continual Arab revolts. Ploughs had to be left, rifles fired. All that on top of illness, ophthalmia, fever, failed crops, inevitable mistakes, and the obstruction of the ever-changing, short-sighted, government officials. The strain of it all, the weariness! The never-ending vigilance!

Even now, though the bad times were over and a dearly bought success had been won, both the farmer and his wife were always up first at the farm. I used to hear them coming and going in the large kitchens on the ground floor preparing the breakfast for the workers. Soon a bell rang, and a moment later workmen filed out on to the road. Vine-growers from Burgundy, ragged Kabyles labourers wearing red tarbooshes; bare-legged Mahonese terrace-builders; Maltese, Lucchese: a whole crowd of mixed nationalities, difficult to manage. Standing at the door and speaking rather abruptly and curtly, the farmer distributed to each of them their task for the day. When he had finished, the good man looked up and anxiously examined the sky; then, seeing me at the window, he called out:

'Bad weather for work in the fields. The sirocco is on its way.'

As the sun rose higher, blasts of suffocating, burning air did indeed begin to come from the south, as if the door of a furnace were opening and closing. You didn't know where to put yourself, what to do. The whole morning passed like this. We had our coffee on the mats out on the gallery, no energy to speak or move. The dogs lay exhausted, stretched out full length, seeking the coolness of the paving-stones. Lunch restored us a little, a strange, lavish meal of carp, trout, boar, hedgehog, Staweli butter, Crescia wines, guavas, bananas, an assortment of dishes as varied as the fruits of nature which surrounded us. Suddenly, outside the French windows, closed to keep from us the furnace-like heat of the garden, there came loud shouts:

'The locusts! The locusts!'

My host went as pale as a man told of some disaster; we rushed outside. The house, till now so silent, was filled for the next ten minutes with the sound of hurrying footsteps, of blurred voices as from people suddenly awakened. From the shade of the corridors where they had been sleeping, servants rushed beating with sticks, forks, flails, on all the metal utensils they could lay their hands on, copper cauldrons, basins, saucepans. The shepherds blew their horns, others blew conch shells and hunting horns. It all made a discordant, frightening din dominated by the shrill 'Yoo! Yoo! Yoo!' of the Arab women come running from the Arab encampment. It seems that often a loud noise, a resounding vibration of the air, is sufficient to prevent the locusts from descending.

But where were these terrible creatures? In the heat-vibrating sky I could see nothing but a compact, copper-coloured cloud approaching on the horizon, like a hail-storm cloud, accompanied by the noise of a gale in the thousand branches of a forest. That cloud was the locusts. Supporting each other with their dry, outstretched wings, they were flying in mass, and, in spite of all our shouts and efforts, the cloud kept on advancing, throwing its immense shadow over the plain. Soon it arrived above our heads; for a second its edges could be seen to become frayed and ragged. Like the beginning of a shower of hail-stones, a few detached themselves, their reddish colour clearly visible. Then the whole cloud burst and, thickly and noisily, this hail-storm of insects fell. As far as the eye could see, the fields were covered with enormous locusts, as big as one's finger.

Then the massacre began. A hideous, grinding, crunching sound, like straw being crushed. The soil, alive with them, was being turned over with harrows, ploughs, mattocks; and the more that were killed, the more there were. They swarmed in layers, their long legs tangled together, those on top leaping painfully into the air, jumping up to the noses of the horses which had been harnessed for this strange work. The farm dogs, those from the Arab encampments, came racing across the fields, hurling themselves on them, pounding them furiously. At the same moment, two companies of Algerian riflemen, buglers at their head, arrived to help the unfortunate colonists, and the method of slaughter changed. Instead of crushing the locusts, the soldiers set fire to them by spreading long trails of gunpowder.

Wearied with the killing, sickened by the foul stench, I went back into the farmhouse. Inside, there were nearly as many as outside. They had entered through gaps in the doors and windows, down the chimneys. They dragged themselves along the edges of the woodwork, into the already eaten curtains, falling, flying, climbing the white walls where they cast gigantic shadows which made them doubly hideous. And always that appalling smell. At dinner, we had to go without water. The cisterns, tanks, wells, fish-ponds, all were tainted. In the evening, in my bedroom, in spite of the large numbers killed there, I could still hear them crawling under the furniture and a cracking of wing-sheaths like the sound of pods bursting in hot weather. There was no sleep again for me that night. But, of course, everybody else spent a sleepless night all over the farm. Flames swept along the ground from one end of the plain to the other. The riflemen kept up their slaughter.

Next day when I opened my window, as I did every morning, the locusts were gone. But the desolation they had left behind them! Not a flower, not a blade of grass, could be seen. Everything was black, barren, and charred. The fruit trees – apricot, banana, peach, mandarin – were recognizable only by the shape of their stripped branches, all their beauty, all that trembling of the leaves which is the life of trees, had gone. The tanks and cisterns were being cleared. Everywhere, labourers were digging the ground to kill the eggs left by the insects. Every clod of earth was being carefully turned over and broken up. And in this upheaval of the fertile earth, thousands of white roots, bursting with sap, were being brought to the surface. It wrung one's heart to see them.

22

Father Gaucher's Elixir

'DRINK this, neighbour, and tell me what you think of it.'

And, drop by drop, with the minute care of a lapidary counting pearls, the priest of the parish of Graveson poured out for me two fingers of an exquisite, sparkling, golden-green liqueur ... It was like a draught of our warm, southern sunshine.

'This is Father Gaucher's elixir, which has brought so much happiness and health to our beloved Provence,' the good man declared proudly. 'They make it at the Monastery of Prémontrés, only a couple of leagues from your mill ... Name me a Chartreuse to equal it; it's worth all of them put together ... The story behind it is so amusing I must tell it you! Listen! . . .'

And, in that presbytery dining-room, so peaceful and innocent with its paintings of the Stations of the Cross and its pretty white curtains starched like surplices, the priest, quite simply and without a trace of guile, told me a story spiced with a certain sceptism and lack of reverence, such as one finds in the tales of Erasmus and Assoucy.

Twenty years ago, the monks of Prémontrés, or the 'White Fathers' as they are called in Provence, had fallen on hard times. If you had seen their monastery in those days you would have been sorry for them. The great outer wall and the Pacôme Tower were falling in ruins. All around the cloisters, which were overgrown with weeds, the pillars were cracking and the stone saints crumbling in their niches. No stained glass remained in the windows, not a door would shut. The Rhône wind swept through the courtyards and the chapels, as it does across the Camargue, blowing out the candles, breaking the lead in the windows, swishing the holy water out of its basins. But the saddest sight of all was the bell-tower, silent as an empty dovecot; and since they had no money to buy a bell, the Fathers had to ring for Matins with castanets made of almond wood! . . .

Poor White Fathers! I can see them still, walking sadly in procession on Corpus Christi in their patched, hooded cloaks, pale and thin and starved-looking, their only food being that which others give to pigs; and walking behind them My Lord Abbott, bowing his head in shame at having to bring his Cross bereft of its gilt, and his worm-eaten mitre, into the light of day for all to see. The ladies of the sisterhood in the procession wept for pity, and the fat banner-bearers jerked their thumbs at the poor monks and sniggered among themselves:

'Brainless birds get thin when they flock together.'

In fact, the unfortunate White Fathers had indeed begun debating among themselves whether it would not be better to disband their order and to go out into the world, each fending for himself.

But one day when this grave question was being discussed in the Chapter House, a message was brought to the Prior that Brother Gaucher wished to be heard by the council. Now this Brother Gaucher was the monastery's cowherd; that is to say, he spent all his time every day wandering slowly round the arcades of the cloisters behind two lean cows which kept searching for the grass between the flagstones. Till the age of twelve he had been brought up by a crazy old woman from the Baux district, known as Aunt Bégon, and then had been taken in by the monks; but this poor cowherd had never been able to learn anything beyond how to herd his cows and to recite his Pater Noster, and even this he said in Provençal, since he was so thick-headed and slow-witted. For the rest, he was a fervent Christian, too fervent even, finding ease in wearing hair-shirts and in disciplining himself with a firm faith and his two arms – and what arms they were!...

When they saw this simple, clumsy-looking man walk into the Chapter House and bow to them all, extending one leg backwards, the whole assembly, Prior, Canons and Treasurer, burst out laughing. But this was the effect which was always produced by his kindly face, his goatee beard, and his rather crazy-looking eyes; and so Brother Gaucher did not let it trouble him.

'Reverend Fathers,' he said, in his innocently good-humoured way, twisting his rosary of olive-stones around his fingers, 'it's quite right, you know, when they say empty barrels make most noise. Because I do believe this empty head of mine has found a way to get us out of all our troubles.

'It's like this. You remember Aunt Bégon, that worthy woman who looked after me when I was little. Ah, yes, what an old rascal she was, God rest her soul! The wicked songs she used to sing after she'd had a few drinks! Yes, well, what I was going to say, Reverend Fathers, was this. Aunt Bégon used to know more about mountain herbs than any old Corsican blackbird. What's more, before she died, she'd brewed up a wonderful elixir, just by mixing together five or six herbs which she and I used to gather upon the Alpilles. That's many a long year ago now, but – with the help of Saint Augustine and the permission of our Father Abbot – I'm sure if I really tried I could find the herbs again that she used for her mysterious elixir. Then all we'd need to do would be to bottle it and sell it at a good price, which would make our community quite rich – like our brothers of La Trappe and La Grande Chartreuse...'

They didn't give him time to finish. The Prior had risen and thrown his arms around his neck. The Canons took him by the hands. The Treasurer, even more excited than the others, started kissing respectfully the tattered edge of his cowl. Then all of them returned to their seats in order to discuss the matter.

Unanimously and without delay the Chapter decided that the cows should be entrusted to Brother Thrasybule, so that Brother Gaucher might be able to devote all his time to the preparation of his elixir.

How did the good brother manage to rediscover Aunt Bégon's recipe? At what cost in effort and in sleepless nights? Nobody can tell us. All we know for certain is that six months later the elixir of the White Fathers was already in great demand. In all the county of Avignon, throughout all the countryside around Arles, there was not a single farmhouse that did not have, at the back of its pantry in between bottles of mulled wine and jars of pickled olives, a little, brown, earthenware flask, sealed with the coat of arms of Provence and carrying a label showing a monk smiling ecstatically. Thanks to the popularity of its elixir, the monastery of Prémontrés became rich very quickly. The Pacôme Tower was restored. The Prior obtained a new mitre, the church some beautiful, stained-glass windows, and within the delicate stone tracery of the bell-tower, a complete peal of bells, large and small, was installed one fine Easter morning and sent forth its clanging, dancing tunes.

As for Brother Gaucher, that poor lay brother whose uncouthness had provided the Chapter with so much merriment, there was no more mention of him in the monastery. Henceforward there was only someone known as the Reverend Father Gaucher, a man of intellect and great learning, who lived completely detached from the numerous, everyday activities of the monastery, shut up from dawn to dusk in his distillery, whilst thirty monks scoured the mountain side, searching for fragrant herbs for him . . . The distillery, which no one – not even the Prior – had the right to enter, was an old, unused chapel at the far end of the Canon's garden. The simple minds of the good Fathers had endowed it with an aura of mystery and awe; and if, by chance, some bold and curious young monk managed by clinging to the creepers to reach the rose-window above the porch, he came down much quicker than he had gone up, overcome with terror at the sight of Father Gaucher, bearded like a necromancer, alcoholometer in hand, surrounded by pink, earthenware retorts, gigantic stills, serpent-like glass tubes: a fantastic conglomeration all glowing through the red of the stained-glass window as if under an enchanter's spell . . .

At the end of the day, as the last Angelus was ringing, the door of this place of mystery used to open unobtrusively, and the Reverend Father would venture forth for the evening service. You should have seen the excitement as he walked through the monastery! The brothers used to line up to see him passing, exclaiming to each other:

'Sh! He's found the secret!'

The Treasurer would follow him, talking to him confidentially . . . In the midst of all this adulation, the Father continued on his way, wiping his forehead, balancing his wide-brimmed, three-cornered hat on the back of his head like a halo, and looking complacently around him at the wide courtyards planted with orange trees, at the blue roofs with their new weather-cocks, and at the Canons in their new robes walking about contentedly in pairs in the now dazzling white cloisters with their elegantly carved pillars.

'I'm the one they owe all this to!' the Reverend Father used to think to himself; and the thought would fill him with pride.

The poor man was heavily punished for this. As you will see . . .

One evening, during the service, he came into the church

in a state of extraordinary agitation: out of breath, red in the face, his hood all askew, and so confused that when he went to dip his fingers in the holy water, he soaked both his sleeves up to the elbows. At first everybody thought he was upset at arriving late; but when he was seen to genuflect reverently several times to the organ and to the galleries instead of before the high altar, tear through the church like a tornado, ramble round the chancel for five minutes trying to find his stall, and then, having found it, to sit bowing his head to the left and then to the right wearing a blissfully happy smile, a murmur of astonishment swept through the church. Everybody whispered to each other behind their breviaries:

'What's the matter with Father Gaucher? . . . What's the matter with Father Gaucher?'

Twice the Prior, losing his patience, banged his crozier on the flagstone to demand silence . . . Away at the far end of the chancel, they had gone on singing the psalms, but the responses became slower and slower . . .

All at once, right in the middle of the *Ave verum*, what does our Father Gaucher do but lean back in his stall and burst forth intoning at the top of his voice:

> 'In Paris a White Father is living!
> Hey! ding-a-ding, Hey! ding-a-ding . . .'

General consternation! Everybody rises. Someone shouts:

'Get him out of here! He's possessed by the devil!'

The Canons make the sign of the Cross! The Prior waves his crozier in the air . . . But Father Gaucher sees nothing, hears nothing, and two brawny monks have to drag him through the little chancel door, struggling as if he were being exorcised and chanting louder than ever his *hey, ding-a-ding*s.

*

The next day, at dawn, the poor man was on his knees in the Prior's oratory, making his confession in a flood of tears:

'It was the elixir, Monsignor, it was the elixir that made me do it,' he kept saying, beating his breast.

And seeing him so contrite and penitent, the good Prior himself was quite affected.

'Come, come, Father Gaucher, calm yourself. It will all pass, like dew in the sunshine . . . After all, the scandal has not been as great as you think. There was that song, of course, which was a little . . . hm! hm! Well, we'll just have to hope the novices did not hear it . . . Now tell me how it all happened . . . It was through testing the elixir, wasn't it? You were a little too generous . . . Yes, yes, I understand . . . Just like Brother Schwarz, the inventor of gunpowder, you became the victim of your own invention . . . But tell me, my good friend, is it really necessary for you to try out this powerful elixir on yourself?'

'Unfortunately, yes, Monsignor. The alcoholometer tells me the strength and the amount of alcohol, but for the final test, for the mellowness, the bouquet, I cannot really trust anything but my own tongue . . .'

'Very well, then . . . Let me ask you one little thing more . . . When you are thus compelled to taste the elixir, do you enjoy it? Does it give you pleasure? . . .'

'Alas, yes, Monsignor,' replied the poor Father, blushing quite red . . . 'The last couple of evenings it has seemed to have a bouquet, an aroma! . . . Oh, it must certainly be the devil who has played this trick on me! So I've made up my mind. In future I shall only use the alcoholometer. It'll be just too bad if the liqueur is not smooth enough, if it's not quite as perfect . . .'

'You'll do no such thing!' interrupted the Prior hastily. 'We must not risk disappointing our customers. All you have to do, now that you have been forewarned, is to be on your guard. Think carefully, how much of it do you need to taste in order to judge it properly? . . . Fifteen to twenty drops about? Let us make it twenty drops. The devil will have to be very clever if he can catch you out with twenty drops . . . What's more, to forestall accidents, I excuse you henceforth from coming to church. You will say your evening devotions in the distillery . . . And now, go in peace, Reverend Father, and remember . . . Take great care to count your drops.'

Alas, poor Father Gaucher could take as much care as he liked over counting his drops, the devil had him in his clutches and wasn't going to let go.

The distillery was to hear some strange devotions!

During the daytime, it must be admitted, everything went well. Father Gaucher kept calm; he prepared his ovens and his stills, carefully sorted out his herbs, the delicate, grey, lace-like herbs of Provence, full of the perfume of our sun-burnt hills . . . But when evening came and the infused herbs had given up their essence and the elixir was cooling in the big red copper pan, the poor man's martyrdom would begin.

'. . . Seventeen . . . eighteen . . . nineteen . . . twenty!'

The drops fell from the glass tube into the ruby-coloured goblet. All twenty of them Father Gaucher used to swallow in one gulp but with scarcely any enjoyment. It was that twenty-first drop he kept wanting. Oh, that twenty-first drop! . . . So, to escape temptation he used to go and kneel at the other end of the laboratory and try to find refuge in his paternosters. But a little aromatic vapour would rise from the still-warm liqueur, and it would come prowling around him and draw him back to his pans in spite of himself . . . The liqueur was a beautiful golden-green . . . Bending over it, inhaling deeply, Father Gaucher would stir it gently with his glass rod, and in the little, sparkling flashes

of light from the swirling, emerald liquid, he seemed to see
the eyes of Aunt Bégon sparkling and laughing at him . . .

'Go on! Just one drop more!'

And one drop leading to the next, the unfortunate man
would end with his goblet full to the brim. Then, all his
resistance overcome, he would let himself fall back into a
large armchair, and, stretching himself voluptuously and
with half-closed eyes, he would sip his sin slowly, savouring

it sensuously, and saying softly to himself with a feeling of exquisite remorse:

'Ah! I shall go to hell for this . . .'

But the most dreadful thing was that at the bottom of his goblet he would always find, by I know not what strange sorcery, all Aunt Bégon's naughty songs:

> 'Three old dames,
> They decided to play games . . .'

or:

> 'Master Andrew's shepherd girl, all on her own,
> Went to the woods – yes, all alone . . .'

and always the same old chorus:

> 'Hey! ding-a-ding; Hey! ding-a-ding . . .'

No wonder he used to feel embarrassed next morning, when the monks in the neighbouring cells would say mischievously:

'Really, Father Gaucher, what a lot of cicadas you must have had in your head when you went to bed last night.'

Then would follow tears, despair, fasting, the hair-shirt and discipline. But nothing could avail against the demon in the elixir: and, every evening, at the same hour, it entered into possession of him again.

Meanwhile, orders kept pouring into the Abbey. They came from Nîmes, from Aix, from Avignon, from Marseilles. Every day the Monastery took on more and more the appearance of a factory. There were packing brothers, labelling brothers, brothers who wrote out the invoices, brothers who drove the delivery carts; with the result that the service of God lost an occasional pull on the bells, but the poor people of the district did not lose by it, I assure you.

But, finally, one beautiful Sunday morning, whilst the Treasurer was reading out his balance-sheet for the past year to a packed Chapter House, and the good Canons were listening with sparkling eyes and smiling lips, Father Gaucher suddenly erupted into the midst of the assembly shouting:

'No more! I've had enough! I've finished with it! I'm not making any more, so give me back my cows!'

'Whatever's the matter, Father Gaucher?' asked the Prior, who'd quite a good idea what the matter was.

'The matter, Monsignor? ... The matter is I'm going the right way to make sure I can look forward to an eternity of flames and little devils pricking me with their forks! ... The matter is I can't stop drinking ... I'm drinking myself straight to Hell! ...'

'But I told you to count your drops.'

'Count my drops! It's goblets I should be counting! Yes, Reverend Father, that's what it's come to. Three full flasks every evening ... I know you'll understand that can't go on ... So get the elixir made by anybody you like ... May the fires of God burn me if I've anything more to do with it!'

The Chapter was no longer smiling!

'But, you wretch, you'll ruin us!' shouted the Treasurer, waving his ledger.

'You'd rather I go to Hell?'

Thereupon the Prior arose.

'Reverend Father,' he said, raising his beautiful white hand on which shone the pastoral ring, 'There is a way of arranging things ... It is in the evening, is it not, my dear son, that the demon tempts you? ...'

'Yes, Monsignor, every evening without fail. It's got so that when I see night coming on, I break out – with all respect to your Reverence – into a cold sweat, like Capitou's donkey when he saw the pack-saddle coming.'

'Well, my son, set your mind at ease ... From now on, at our service every evening, we shall say for your benefit the prayer of Saint Augustine, to which a plenary indulgence is attached. With that, whatever happens you will be covered . . . It gives you absolution even in the act of sinning.'

'Oh, good, that's all right then! Thank you, Monsignor!' And without further question, Father Gaucher went back to his stills, light-hearted as a lark.

Sure enough, from that moment on, every evening at the end of compline, the officiating Father never failed to say:

'Let us pray for our poor Father Gaucher, who is sacrificing himself in the interests of the community . . . *Oremus Domine* . . .'

And whilst above all those white cowls bent low in the darkness of the naves, that prayer swept soughing like a small icy blast of winter over the white snow, down there at the far end of the monastery, behind the glowing-red windows of the distillery, you could hear Father Gaucher singing at the top of his voice:

> 'In Paris a White Father is living,
> Hey! ding-a-ding, Hey! ding-a-ding;
> In Paris a White Father is living:
> The little nuns dance, at his command,
> All round the garden hand-in-hand,
> Hey! ding-a-ding, Hey! ding-a-ding . . .'

Here the worthy parish-priest stopped petrified:
'Oh, mercy on me! Suppose my parishioners heard me!'

23

In the Camargue

1. *The Departure*

GREAT rejoicing in the château. A messenger dispatched by the gamekeeper has announced, in a mixture of French and Provençal, that there have already been two or three good flights of ducks and snipe, and that numerous other birds are arriving early.

'You are one of us!' my kindly neighbours have written; so, at five o'clock this morning, their big wagonette laden with guns, dogs and food came to pick me up at the foot of the hill. And here we are on this December morning, racing along the dry and rather barren-looking road to Arles, the pale green of the olive trees scarcely yet visible and the loud garish green of the Kernes oaks looking a little too artificially wintry. The cowsheds are stirring. Lights in farm windows tell of people already up and working, and in niches among the stones of the Abbey of Montmajour, sea-hawks still half-asleep flap their wings among the ruins. We begin to pass old peasant women on their way to market, trotting along on their little donkeys at the side of the road. They come from Ville-des-Baux. Six long leagues in order to sit for an hour on the steps of Saint-Trophyme and sell their little bundles of herbs gathered on the mountains! . . .

Now come the ramparts of Arles; low, crenellated walls such as one sees in old prints showing warriors armed with lances on top of sloping ramps not as big as themselves. We pass at a gallop through this wonderful little town, one of the most picturesque in France, with its rounded carved balconies projecting into the middle of the narrow streets, like those in Arab countries, and old, dark houses with little arched doors in the Moorish style, which recall the days of William Short-Nose and the Saracens. At this hour there is still nobody about. Only on the quai beside the Rhône is there a bustling of activity. The steamer that makes the trip to the Camargue is getting up steam ready for its departure.

Farmers in short jackets of russet woollen twill, girls from La Roquette wanting to hire themselves out for farm work, go aboard with us, laughing and talking among themselves. Underneath their long hooded, brown cloaks, drawn tight against the chill of the morning, their high *arlésienne* coiffure makes their faces seem small and elegant, with an appealing impudence, an air of roguish laughter. The bell rings; we are off. Our speed is tripled by the Rhône, the screw and the mistral, and the banks fly past on either side. On one is La Crau, a dry, stony plain. On the other, the Camargue: greener, with short grass and marshes full of reeds extending to the sea.

From time to time, the boat stops at a landing-stage, on the left or on the right, at the Empire or the Kingdom, as they used to say in the Middle Ages in the days of the Royal Kingdom of Arles, and as the old watermen on the Rhône still say to this day. At each stop there is a white farmhouse, a clump of trees. The workmen go ashore carrying their tools; the women walk erect down the gangway, their baskets on their arms. Between Empire and Kingdom, little by little the boat empties and there is scarcely anybody left on board when it arrives at the landing-stage at Mas-de-Giraud where we get off.

Mas-de-Giraud is an old farmhouse of the lords of Barbentane, and it is here that we await the arrival of the gamekeeper who is to come to fetch us. In its kitchen all the men of the farm, labourers, vine-tenders, shepherds, are seated at table, solemn, silent, eating slowly, served by the women who will not eat until afterwards. Soon the game-keeper arrives with the small cart. He is a real Fennimore Cooper character, a trapper on land and water, gamekeeper and fishing-warden. The local people call him 'The Prowler' because he is always to be seen in the dawn or evening mists lying in hide-outs among the reeds or else sitting motionless in his little boat watching his lines in the pools and channels. Perhaps it is this occupation of eternal watcher that renders him so silent, so self-contained. However, while the cart piled high with guns and baskets moves on ahead of us, he gives us the latest news, the number of flights, the places where the migrating birds have descended. As we talk of these matters, we penetrate deeper and deeper into the Camargue.

As far as the eye can see, stretches this wild land of marshes and channels gleaming between pastures and clumps of marsh grass. Reeds and tufts of tamarisk appear to float like little islands on a calm sea. Not a tall tree is to be seen. The immense flat expanse stretches unbroken. Far away in the distance, the occasional roof of a cattle-shed appears to be almost level with the ground. Scattered herds, lying in the salt grass, or wandering around a russet-coated herdsman, do not disturb the great straight line of the horizon beneath the high blue sky. As from the sea, level in spite of its waves, there arises from this vast plain a feeling of solitude, of infinite spaces, a feeling that is increased by the mistral which blows unimpeded and unceasing and with such power that it seems to make this vast, flat land even more flat and even more vast. Everything bends before it. The smallest bushes near the imprint of its passage, remaining forever bowed and twisted, leaning southwards as if in an attitude of perpetual flight . . .

II. *The Hut*

A roof of reeds, walls of reeds – dry, yellow reeds: that is the hut. And such is our base for the shoot. Typical of the Camargue, the hut consists of a single vast windowless room into which the daylight enters only through the glazed door which is covered at night with heavy shutters. Along the whole length of the white-washed, rough-cast walls are racks for the guns, for the game bags, for the high boots for the marshes. At the far end, five or six cots are ranged around a real mast planted in the soil and rising to the roof which it supports. At night when the mistral blows and the hut creaks all over, the wind brings with it the sound, magnified to a roar, of the distant sea, and then one could imagine oneself lying in a bunk in a ship's cabin.

But it is in the afternoons the hut is at its best. During the beautiful days of our southern winter, I love to stay near the high fireplace on which a few tamarisk roots are smouldering. Under the force of the mistral or of the tramontane, the door shakes, the reeds shriek, yet these noises are only tiny echoes of the howling uproar of Nature all around me. The winter sunshine, lashed by powerful blasts, is dispersed and scattered, only to be flickeringly united and scattered again. Great shadows race across the land beneath a sky of incredible blue. The light comes in spasms, the sounds also; and the cowbells, suddenly heard, then forgotten, lost in the wind, return tunefully under the shaking door like a charming refrain . . . The most exquisite hour is twilight, just before the guns return. Then the wind has calmed. I go out for a moment. The great red sun is peacefully descending, fiery, without warmth. Night is falling, lightly brushing you in passing with her moist, black wing. Over there, close to the ground, the flash of a gunshot blazes with the brilliance of a red star made more brilliant by the surrounding darkness. In what remains of the day, life quickens. A long triangle of ducks comes flying very low, as if they want to descend; but suddenly the hut, in which the lamp is now lit, scares them off; the leader of the column raises his neck, rises again, and all behind him follow uttering wild cries.

Soon an immense pattering, like the sound of rain, is heard approaching. Gathered in by the shepherds, driven by the racing, panting dogs, thousands of timid confused sheep are crowding towards the folds. I am surrounded, jolted, overwhelmed by this moving mass of bleating fleece: a surging, swaying flood which appears to carry both the shepherds and their long shadows on the surface of a succession of mounting waves . . . Behind the flocks come familiar steps, happy voices. The logs flare up. Everybody laughs more when tired, light-headed with happy lassitude. Guns are put in a corner, high boots hurled in all directions; emptied bags are thrown down and beside them are placed the birds, their red, gold, green and silver feathers stained with blood. The table is laid; and amongst the steam rising from bowls of rich eel soup, silence falls again, the grand silence of healthy appetites, interrupted only by the ferocious growl of the dogs, as in the darkness outside the door they lap gropingly from their basins . . .

The evening will be short. Already, near the fire, itself almost asleep, there remain only the gamekeeper and myself. We talk, that is we throw a word at each other now and then as peasants do: Red Indian grunts which fade away as quickly as the dying sparks of the smouldering embers. At last the gamekeeper gets up, lights his lantern, and I listen to his heavy footsteps fading into the night . . .

III. *On Chance* (*The Hide-out*)

On chance! An apt name to give to the hide-out, the waiting place of the hidden hunter, and to the uncertain hours between dawn and dusk spent waiting and hesitating, *on chance*. Long hours they are, crouched in the hide-out from before the rising of the sun until its setting. It is the latter I prefer, especially in these marsh lands where the daylight lingers for so long on the waters of the pools.

Sometimes the hide-out is a small narrow keel-less boat, which rolls at the slightest movement. Hidden by the reeds, the hunter crouches at the bottom of the boat watching for the ducks; all that can be seen is the peak of a cap, the barrel of a gun, and the head of a dog who sniffs the wind and snaps at the mosquitoes, sometimes making the boat sway and fill with water by stretching out his big paws. I lack the experience for that sort of hide-out. So mostly I go *on chance* on foot, paddling about far out in the marshes in enormous, tall leather boots. I walk slowly and carefully for fear of getting stuck in the mud. I push back the brackish-smelling reeds full of jumping frogs . . .

At last I reach a tiny island of tamarisk, a little piece of dry land where I make myself at home. To make me feel more like a hunter, the gamekeeper has lent me his dog, an enormous dog from the Pyrenees with a thick, white coat, a first-class hunting dog, by whose presence I am more than a little intimidated. When a water-hen passes within my range, he has a certain ironical way of looking at me, throwing back with an artistic toss of the head his long, limp ears that hang down over his eyes; then his nose points, his tail wags, as if saying impatiently:

'Fire!... Fire, can't you!'

I fire. I miss. Then languidly stretching himself out at full length, he yawns with dumb insolence.

All right, yes! I admit it, I am a poor hunter. The hide-out, for me, means the coming of night; the light fading, hiding itself on the water, on the gleaming pools, polishing to a fine silvery tone the darkening grey of the sky. I love the strange smell of the water, the mysterious rustling of the insects among the reeds, the faint murmuring of the long, quivering leaves. Every now and then a sound, sad as the soft booming of a sea-shell, fills the sky. It is the bittern, plunging his immense fishing beak into the water and, blowing... rrroo... oooo! Flights of crane file overhead. I hear the swishing of their feathers, the ruffling of the down in the keen air, and even the creaking of their little tired bones. Then, nothing more; night deepens, and only a faint trace of daylight remains on the waters...

Suddenly I feel a shudder run through me, a sort of nervous thrill, as if I knew there was somebody behind me. I turn, and I see that companion of beautiful nights, the moon, an immense moon, quite round, rising gently, its movement noticeable at first and then less so as it rises higher above the horizon.

Already the first moonbeams are lighting land and water and soon the whole marsh shines bright in the moonlight. The smallest tuft of grass has its shadow. The hide-out is finished, the birds see us: it is time to go. The way back is a walk through light, through a flood of soft, dusty-blue light; and each step taken in the pools and channels disturbs crowds of fallen stars and moonbeams which are descending deep, deep into the water.

IV. *Red and White*

Quite close to us, a gun-shot from the hut, there is another hut, similar but more rustic. It is there that our game-keeper lives with his wife and his two elder children: a daughter who makes the meals for the men and mends the fishing nets, and a boy who helps his father lift the lines and watch the sluice gates of the ponds. His two younger children are at Arles with their grandmother; they will stay with her until they have learnt to read and have taken their first Communion, for here it is too far from a church or a school, and also the air of the Camargue is not good for little ones. In summer, in fact, when the marshes are dry and the white mud of the channels cracks in the great heat, the island is really quite uninhabitable.

I saw it like that once, in the month of August, when I came to shoot young wild duck, and I shall never forget the gloomy ferocity of this burnt-out land. Everywhere the pools were steaming under the sun like immense cauldrons, their beds still alive with the remnants of life, wriggling salamanders, spiders, water-flies, all seeking moist corners. Over it all there floated an air of pestilence, a steaming, heavy noxious mist, made even thicker by the innumerable whirling clouds of mosquitoes. Everyone in the game-keeper's house was shaking with fever, and it was pitiful to see the faces, haggard and yellow, and the eyes, dark-ringed and too large, of these unfortunate people condemned to exist, for three whole months, beneath that merciless sun which burnt their fevered bodies without warming them . . . Sad and painful is the life of a gamekeeper in the Camargue! Still, this one has his wife and his children near him; but two leagues away in the marsh there is a horse-keeper who lives, quite alone from one year to the next, as if he were on a desert island. In his hut of reeds, which he built himself, there is not a thing he has not made himself, from the plaited wicker hammock, the black, stone fireplace, the stools carved from tamarisk roots, to the lock and key of white wood with which he secures his strange dwelling.

The man himself is as strange as his dwelling place. He is a kind of philosopher, silent like all solitary people, hiding his peasant wariness under thick, bushy eyebrows. When he is not on his grazing pasture, he is to be found seated in front of his door, puzzling out slowly, and with touching, child-like concentration, one of the pink, blue or yellow pamphlets with which the chemist wraps the medicaments he uses for his horses. The poor devil has no other distraction except reading, and these are all that he has to read. Although they are neighbours, our gamekeeper and he do not see each other. They even avoid meeting. One day I asked The Prowler the reason for this antipathy and he answered gravely:

'It's because of our opinions ... He is red, and I am white.'

Thus, even in this barren solitude, where loneliness should have brought them together, these two men of the wilds, each as simple-minded and as ignorant as the other, these two herdsmen out of Theocritus who go to town scarcely once a year and for whom the little cafés of Arles with their gilt mirrors possess the dazzling splendours of the palaces of the Ptolemies, have found a means of hating each other in the name of their political beliefs!

v. *The Vaccarès*

The most beautiful part of all the Camargue is the Vaccarès. Many times, after leaving the others to their sport, have I come to sit on the banks of this salt-water lake, this inland sea, which, by being shut off from the ocean, seems by the very fact of its captivity to have become more familiar and more friendly. In place of that lifeless aridity which tends so often to give a cheerless aspect to the sea-coast, the high banks of the Vaccarès, with their fine, green velvety sward display a variety of beautiful and unusual flora: centauries, marsh-trefoils, gentians, and the pretty behen, blue in winter, red in summer, changing its colour with the changing atmosphere, and registering the passage of the seasons with the diverse tints of its perennial blossoms.

Towards five o'clock in the evening, when the sun is beginning to set, these three leagues of water with not a boat or a sail breaking their vast expanse have a wonderful charm. It is not the more intimate charm of the pools and channels, seen here and there in the distance between folds of marshy earth beneath which one senses the water seeping along, seeking to surface in the slightest declivity. Here the impression is of largeness and grandeur.

From far-off, the sparkling glitter of the waves attracts flocks of ducks, heron, bittern, and white-breasted, rose-winged flamingoes, all lining the banks in order to fish, their varied colours distributed evenly in a long ribbon; and then the ibis, the real ibis from Egypt, so completely at home beneath the splendid sun of this silent land. Indeed, from where I am sitting, I can hear no sound, save the lapping of the water and the voice of the keeper calling to his horses scattered along the lake-side. They all have resounding names: 'Cifer! . . . (Lucifer) . . . L'Estello! . . . L'Estour-nello! . . .' Each horse, on hearing its name, comes trotting up with its mane flying in the wind, and eats the oats out of its keeper's hands . . .

Further off, on the same bank, there is a large herd of cattle grazing freely like the horses. Now and then, above the clumps of tamarisk, I see their curved backs and their little crescent-shaped horns. Most of these cattle of the

Camargue are raised for baiting at the village festivals, and some have names already famous in all the arenas of Provence and Languedoc. Thus the herd nearest me contains, among others, a fierce fighter called '*Le Romain*', who has gored I don't know how many men and horses in the arenas of Arles, Nîmes and Tarascon. For that reason his companions have accepted him as their leader; since among these strange herds the animals govern themselves, grouping themselves around an old bull whom they have adopted as leader. When a hurricane sweeps across the Camargue, a terrifying thing on this wide plain where there is nothing to stop it or turn it aside, you should see the herd huddle together behind its leader, all their heads lowered, turning to the wind those wide foreheads where their massive strength is concentrated. Our Provençal shepherds call this manoeuvre: '*vira la bano au giscle*' – turning the horns to the wind. And all the worse for the herd that does not carry it out! Blinded by the rain, swept away by the hurricane, the routed herd panics and scatters, and the demented beasts, racing headlong to escape the storm, fling themselves into the Rhône, into the Vaccarès or into the sea.

24

Barrack-room Memories

I AM awakened this morning startlingly at the first light of dawn by the tremendous beating of a drum . . . Rat-a-tat-tat! Rat-a-tat-tat!

A drum beating in my pine trees at his hour! . . . That, certainly, is something out of the ordinary.

I quickly leap out of bed and run to open the door.

Nobody to be seen! The row has ceased . . . From among the wild vines wet with dew a few curlews rise shaking their wings . . . A slight northerly wind sighs among the trees . . . To the east on the peaks of the Lesser Alps hangs a mist, like gold dust, through which the sun is slowly appearing. Its first rays are already touching the roof of the mill. At the same time, the invisible drum begins to beat the general salute . . . Rat-a-tat-tat! Tat! Tat!

What sort of savage is it who comes into the middle of a pinewood to salute the dawn with a drum? . . . I look round in every direction but see nothing . . . nothing except the tufts of lavender and the pine trees tumbling down the slope to the road far below. Perhaps, down there in the bushes, some impish sprite is hiding having a good laugh at me . . . Ariel, perhaps, or Master Puck. When he's been passing my mill, the rascal's said to himself:

'That Parisian is too quiet in there. We'll give him a little surprise.'

Whereupon he must have got hold of a big drum and . . . Rat-a-tat-tat! . . . Rat-a-tat-tat! . . . Will you be quiet, Puck, you rascal! You'll waken my cicadas.

*

It wasn't Puck.

It was Gouguet François, known as 'Pistolet', drummer of the 31st of the line, and at the moment on his six months' leave of absence. Pistolet gets bored with the country; he has nostalgic memories, this drummer, and – when someone is good enough to lend him the village drum – off he goes gloomily into the woods and bangs away at it, dreaming all the time of the Prince-Eugène Barracks.

Today it is on my little green hill that he has come to dream ... He is there, standing beside a pine, his drum between his legs, drumming away to his heart's content ... Coveys of startled partridges fly up from under his feet without his noticing them. All around Nature fills the air with delightful scents, without his noticing them.

Nor does he notice the frail spiders' webs trembling between the branches in the sunshine, nor the pine needles leaping up and down on his drum. Lost entirely in his dream and in his music, he watches his flying drum-sticks with loving eyes, and his big, simple face beams with pleasure at each roll of the drum.

Rat-a-tat-tat! Rat-a-tat-tat!

'Oh, how beautiful is the big barracks, its courtyard with its large paving-stones, its rows and rows of windows, its men all in forage-caps, and its low archways full of the noise of mess-tins!'

Rat-a-tat-tat! Rat-a-tat-tat!

'Oh, its echoing staircases, its white-washed corridors, its smelly dormitories, the belts to polish, the bread boards, the jars of polish, the iron cots with their grey blankets, the rifles glittering in the racks!'

Rat-a-tat-tat! Rat-a-tat-tat!

'Oh, those good days in the guard-house, the playing-cards that stick to the fingers, the hideous Queen of Spades with embellishments in ink, the old, odd volume of Pigault-Lebrun!'*

Rat-a-tat-tat! Rat-a-tat-tat! . . .

'Oh, the long nights on sentry duty at the doors of the Ministries, the old sentry box that leaks, the feet that are always cold! . . . The fine carriages that splash you with mud as they pass! . . . Oh, the extra fatigues, the days confined to barracks, the stinking bucket, the plank for a pillow, the cold reveille on rainy mornings, the foggy "retreat" when the gas lamps are lit, and arriving running, out of breath, at the evening roll-calls!' . . .

Rat-a-tat-tat! Rat-a-tat-tat! . . .

'Oh, the *Bois de Vincennes*, the big white cotton gloves, the walks on the fortifications . . . Oh, the gate of the *École Militaire*, the soldiers' sweethearts, the *cornet-à-piston* of the *Salon de Mars*,† absinthe in the music-halls, confidences between hiccups, swords unsheathed, and the sentimental ballad sung with one's hand upon one's heart! . . .'

Dream, poor fellow, dream! It is not for me to stop

---

*The author of some rather bawdy books (1753–1835).
†Dancing rooms near the Champs de Mars.

you ... beat your drum with all your might, beat it with your whirling arms. I have no right to laugh at you.

If you have your nostalgic barrack-room memories, have I not mine also?

My Paris haunts me here, just as your does. You play a drum beneath the pines! I ... I prepare my copy for the Paris newspapers ... Ah, what fine sons of Provence we are! Up there, in the barrack-rooms of Paris, we sigh for the blue of our Little Alps and the wild scent of their lavender; and now, here, in the very heart of Provence, we miss our barrack-rooms, and everything that reminds us of them is dear to us! ...

Eight o'clock strikes in the village, Pistolet, still whirling his drum-sticks, is marching homewards ... I hear him descending through the pines, still playing ... And it seems to me, as I lie in the grass, aching with the pain of my memories, that I am seeing, in the sound of that receding drum, all my Paris, passing between the pines ...

Oh, Paris! ... Paris! ... Always Paris!

MORE ABOUT PENGUINS, PELICANS
AND PUFFINS

For further information about books available from Penguins please write to Dept EP Penguin Books Ltd, Harmondsworth, Middlesex UB7 0DA.

In the U.S.A.: For a complete list of books available from Penguins in the United States write to Dept DG, Penguin Books, 299 Murray Hill Parkway, East Rutherford, New Jersey 07073.

In Canada: For a complete list of books available from Penguins in Canada write to Penguin Books Canada Ltd, 2801 John Street, Markham, Ontario L3R 1B4.

In Australia: For a complete list of books available from Penguins in Australia write to the Marketing Department, Penguin Books Australia Ltd, P.O. Box 257, Ringwood, Victoria 3134.

In New Zealand: For a complete list of books available from Penguins in New Zealand write to the Marketing Department, Penguin Books (N.Z.) Ltd, P.O. Box 4019, Auckland 10.

In India: For a complete list of books available from Penguins in India write to Penguin Overseas Ltd, 706 Eros Apartments, 56 Nehru Place, New Delhi 110019.

FLAUBERT

—

THREE TALES

Translated by Robert Baldick

With *Madame Bovary* Flaubert established the realistic
novel. Twenty years later he wrote the *Three Tales*, each of
which reveals a different aspect of his creative genius and fine
craftsmanship. In *A Simple Heart*, a story set in his native
Normandy, he recounts the life of a pious and devoted
servant-girl. A stained-glass window in Rouen cathedral in-
spired him to write *The Legend of St Julian Hospitator* with
its insight into the violence and mysticism of the medieval
mind. *Herodias*, the last of the three, is a masterly recon-
struction of the events leading up to the martyrdom of St
John the Baptist.

SENTIMENTAL EDUCATION

Translated by Robert Baldick

'I know nothing more noble', wrote Flaubert, 'than the
contemplation of the world.' His acceptance of all the realities
of life (rather than his remorseless exposure of its illusions)
principally recommends what many regard as a more mature
work than *Madame Bovary*, if not the greatest French novel
of the last century. In Robert Baldick's new translation of
this story of a young man's romantic attachment to an older
woman, the modern reader can appreciate the accuracy, the
artistry, and the insight with which Flaubert (1821–80) re-
constructed in one masterpiece the very fibre of his times.

and

MADAME BOVARY
BOUVARD AND PÉCUCHET
SALAMMBO